Ecstasy Romance

"GET THAT LOOK OUT OF YOUR EYES, SAM CHASE," JOANNA SAID WITH A WARNING GLINT.

"I don't want to know what your fantasies are about city women, because I'm going to be too busy learning about survival to get caught up in—"

He cocked his head, his expression definitely smug. "I only handed you a compliment, not a place in my bed. Slow down. I like to get to know a lady before I get serious."

"Oh, and is bedding a woman serious business to you?" Joanna flung back.

"Up here in the country we take our romancing very seriously. There aren't that many gorgeous women to go around, so we've got to select carefully."

"Pity," she said. "I'm not in the market for romance."

"That is a pity, but then again, you might change your mind. Women are known to do that."

CANDLELIGHT ECSTASY ROMANCES®

A MATTER OF STYLE

Alison Tyler

A CANDLELIGHT ECSTASY ROMANCE®

Published by
Dell Publishing Co., Inc.
1 Dag Hammarskjold Plaza
New York, New York 10017

Dell ® TM 681510, Dell Publishing Co., Inc.
Candlelight Ecstasy Romance®, 1,203,540, is a registered
trademark of Dell Publishing Co., Inc., New York,
New York.

ISBN: 0-440-15305-0

Printed in the United States of America

First printing—March 1985

To Our Readers:

We have been delighted with your enthusiastic response to Candlelight Ecstasy Romances®, and we thank you for the interest you have shown in this exciting series.

In the upcoming months we will continue to present the distinctive sensuous love stories you have come to expect only from Ecstasy. We look forward to bringing you many more books from your favorite authors and also the very finest work from new authors of contemporary romantic fiction.

As always, we are striving to present the unique, absorbing love stories that you enjoy most—books that are more than ordinary romance. Your suggestions and comments are always welcome. Please write to us at the address below.

Sincerely,

The Editors
Candlelight Romances
1 Dag Hammarskjold Plaza
New York, New York 10017

CHAPTER ONE

"Does anybody have some aspirin?" Joanna Winfield muttered, tossing her appointment book, hairbrush, Gucci wallet, and a dozen loose papers back into her tote bag. "I must have used the rest of mine yesterday."

"Slow down, Jo. You're going to give yourself an ulcer one of these days." Gary Simms handed the distraught young woman a lipstick tube that had fallen in her mad search for relief.

"Tell me something, Gary. Who in this crazy business of ours doesn't have at least one ulcer? I feel guilty that mine isn't even in the running."

"It will be, sweetheart—if you keep it up."

"Thanks, Gary. You know how to cheer up a poor working girl." Joanna smiled affectionately as she tossed the lipstick into her bag.

Sue Peters slid a tin of aspirin down the conference table to Joanna.

"It's comforting that someone here comes prepared," Joanna quipped, popping two tablets into her mouth, expertly swallowing them with one gulp of water. "Now, let's wrap this one up. For the most part Robeson likes the idea of Cinderfella getting doused with some Mirage by a sexy fairy godmother. But he still wants more flash—that is, more 'broads'—in the ad."

Joanna smiled as the five people sitting around the table groaned in unison.

"Hasn't Robeson heard of the new Antisexist League that forbids more than one 'buxom broad' per ad?" Caroline Gray asked with a sneer.

"No—and neither have I, for that matter." Joanna grinned.

"Well, I think I'll start one."

"Good idea. But first redo the ad layout and give our well-paying client all the flash his heart desires. Unless, of course, we decide to join the unemployment lines."

Actually that idea had been sounding more and more appealing to Joanna in recent months. She shook her head clear of the notion. Lately she'd had fantasies of escaping the whole kit and caboodle—the ad agency job that nurtured her up-and-coming ulcer, the daily A.M. and P.M. subway rush warfare, the three-room apartment that looked out on a paint-cracked sky blue air shaft, and a social life in which all the men she met either turned out to be married or else had some telling reasons they'd remained on the market. A few months ago Joanna had sworn off singles bars. That left parties and blind dates, invariably peopled with the same men who in their off nights attended the singles bars she was diligently avoiding.

Joanna knew she was becoming overly cynical

and too critical where men were concerned. It wasn't as if she were on a desperate search for a husband. All she wanted was a pleasant, uncomplicated meaningful relationship. Lately, though, she had begun to feel that the whole process of looking for Mr. All Right was not worth the effort. And when it came down to the nitty-gritty, Joanna was fast drawing the conclusion that she no longer knew what she wanted. She knew only what she didn't want. Unfortunately she was in no position to walk out of a good-paying job as an advertising exec in one of the best agencies in New York City to go "find herself."

"You look beat, Jo." Gary had stayed behind while the others shuffled out grumbling about the extra hours they all would have to put in that night.

"Why are you on my case today, Gary?" Joanna gave her assistant an affectionate poke.

Gary pulled up a chair beside her and took her hand. "Because next to my wife, my three kids, and my dear old mom, I love you, babe."

Joanna smiled. "How come all the good guys are happily married?" Stretching, she leaned back in her chair and yawned. "I am beat."

"You need a vacation—some lush island in the Bahamas where you can have yourself a ball."

"I don't want to have a ball. I want quiet. I want peace, tranquillity, rolling meadows, silent walks along a country path, starry nights, crisp days—"

11

"Okay already." He laughed. "I get the picture."

"You know what I want, Gary?"

"Isn't that what you've just been telling me?"

"No. Are you ready to hear what I'd really love to do?" She squinted warily at him. "Promise not to laugh."

"You are too brilliant for me to laugh at any of your ideas, Jo. That's why you're in the chair and I'm contentedly sitting at your feet," he said with a good-natured smile.

"Here's my dream. You remember that cabin in Vermont I stayed at for a week last summer?"

"The one with creaking floors, raccoons in the attic, an old outhouse—"

"It wasn't an outhouse. Only the shower was outside. And the guy who owned the place was planning to build a new indoor shower." She sat forward, hands on her chin. Her shoulder-length copper hair fell loosely around her face. The startling color of her hair set against the flawless, milky complexion of her classic cheekbones reminded Gary once again that Joanna Winfield was a gorgeous woman with a terrific head on her shoulders as well. With these assets going for her, Joanna should not be feeling miserable. But when she turned to face him, those gray-green eyes of hers were brimming with tears.

"I don't know what's wrong with me lately. Almost any woman would give her right arm to be in my shoes, and all I can think about is running barefoot in daffodil-covered meadows.

Chuck Harvey—that's the guy with the cabin—dropped me a note last week to say he was thinking about selling the place this winter, so if I wanted to come up again before then, I should call him."

"That sounds like a great idea. Take a week off and go up there, run around the hills and dales, see the glories of a New England autumn—"

"I want to buy the place," Joanna interrupted.

"Sure, why not?" he said lightly but Joanna's unsmiling glance told him instantly she was serious. "Come on, Jo. What would you do with a beat-up cabin in Vermont?"

"Live in it."

"Oh, I see. Sure, of course. And tell me, what would you live on: nature's fruits?"

"That's the part I haven't figured out yet. Maybe I'll win on that sweepstakes ticket I bought this week." She sighed. "Or—who knows?—maybe someone I've never heard of will die and leave me some of their leftover millions. But between now and then I really could buy the place; my little nest egg would cover a down payment."

"That leaves only the mortgage, gas and electricity, and eating," Gary pointed out.

"The place has a wood stove. If my ancestors could chop firewood, so can I. But eating—that's not so easy. In the summertime there's always a garden. And I could raise chickens. I had an uncle who ran a chicken farm. Maybe it's a talent that runs in the family."

"Jo, Jo. Stop. You're beginning to make me

nervous. You sound too serious. We need you here at good old Bailey and Johnson. Who else would have come up with Cinderfella or the zillion other brilliant ideas you've had?"

"Fifty other bright, ambitious women just waiting to be asked."

"No way. You underestimate that mind of yours."

"This mind of mine feels like mush lately. My body, too," she grumbled, patting a nonexistent tummy. "The only exercise I've gotten in the last few months is bending down to pick up spilled aspirin."

Gary took hold of her hands. "Joanna, you're nuts. You are a first-class beauty with a superb body. . . . Remind me to take flowers home to Julie for my lascivious thoughts."

"I'm too far gone for flattery."

"You need a man—"

"Stop right there, Mr. Simms. I do not need a man of any kind, so don't try that angle. Men are half my problem. I am sick and tired of the whole dating scene. First date, you're miserably disappointed, or you have to practice a couple of karate maneuvers to get the guy off your doorstep, or he's terrific except for the fact that he happens to have a wife at home who doesn't understand him. And the second date—usually it's another first date."

"You're exaggerating. What about Brad Harper? You two had a good thing going there for a while."

Joanna gave him a rueful nod. "Oh, yes, let's

14

not forget dear Brad. Our good thing, as you called it, required me to pretend I was an idiot. Shall we just say that Brad had some problems with competition. Never go out with another adman. Remember that, Gary."

He chuckled. "That's one I think I can keep in mind. But seriously, Jo, there've got to be a few guys out there worth their weight in gold."

"I guess so. But I, for one, am tired of panning for gold. Here I am, twenty-nine years old— thirty next year. For years I've been trying to convince myself—as *Ms* magazine keeps telling me—that I don't need a man in order to be happy and fulfilled. Well, I'm finally convinced. The best thing I can do for myself is decide to depend on nobody but little old me. I'll tell you, Gary, I'm tired of the whole rat race, including the Bailey and Johnson Advertising Agency."

"The pay's good."

"That's why I'm still hanging in. If I could figure out some way to survive in that little cabin of my dreams, I'd go tomorrow. And stay for at least a year. Just to see what it would be like to think about nothing but gathering eggs, chopping wood, reading by candlelight—"

"Candlelight?"

"Abe Lincoln did it."

"You planning to come back from survival training and run for President?"

"I know you think my whole idea is crazy. Don't think I haven't considered that possibility myself."

"Good." Gary stood up and kissed her lightly

15

on the forehead before he retrieved his brown leather briefcase. "Those are the first sane words I've heard from you about this cabin nonsense. Go home and relax, Jo. Tomorrow is a new day."

Gary Simms could never have guessed just how new the next day would be. When Joanna returned home, two fateful letters were waiting in her mailbox. They both looked official, and the return addresses were unfamiliar. Joanna waited until she got upstairs to open them.

When she finished reading the first one, she almost didn't bother opening the second, deciding it might be wiser to spread bad news over a couple of days. She was fuming. The letter informed her that her three-room apartment—which already cost her more than it was worth—was now going to cost an additional one hundred a month more than it was worth.

"This is outright robbery," she muttered. "They can't do this." She sat down on the couch. "Yes, they can." She looked about the living room. It was small, but she had done a lot with it: a classy Berber tweed carpet; sleek contemporary furniture; a couple of well-chosen bold geometric paintings on the eggshell white walls. Somehow, looking at the place right now, Joanna decided it all looked phony, sterile, dull. And damn well not worth another hundred bucks. Then again, what choice did she have? Finding a decent, affordable apartment in Manhattan was even harder than finding a decent

16

man. Joanna knew that the same woman ready to pounce on her job would also grab up this apartment as a real find, rent increase and all.

She walked into her bedroom, the bed still unmade from this morning. Without thinking, she started to shake out the quilt. She stopped in mid-shake. What was the point? She'd be getting into bed in a few hours anyway.

Bad sign, she said to herself. *Should try to keep up appearances. To hell with appearances.* Joanna came to the conclusion, staring at her half-made bed, that she was living a cardboard life in a cardboard world. She laughed. Good sign—at least she could still see some humor in it all. She walked back into the living room and picked up the second envelope.

After she had read the letter once, she sat down on the couch and read it again. And again. Placing the sheet of paper on her lap, she took a deep breath.

An hour ago she had been fantasizing about winning the lottery, and now something even more unbelievable was happening. She had almost forgotten about that bus accident on Thirty-fourth and Madison, but the letter reminded her it had occurred almost two years ago to the day. On that particular morning Joanna had decided to avoid the subway rush and try the bus for a change of scene. This turned out not to be a wise decision, although, sitting on her couch now, letter in her trembling hands, she realized it had probably been the luckiest day of her life. A crazy cabby had overshot a turn and sideswiped the bus, causing a minor crash that nonetheless left in its wake some sprains, bruises, and broken bones. Joanna was one of the passengers on the bus who had suffered all three.

She remembered her lawyer's telling her never to choose the city to sue. Joanna explained that it wasn't a matter of choice. He filed for her, informing her that she probably wouldn't get any response for five years or more. It would take that long for the suit to be heard, and in his opinion the insurance company was unlikely to settle out of court.

He had been wrong. Joanna hugged the letter against her breast. Who said miracles don't happen? Had Gary been sitting in that room with her at that moment, he would have been really nervous. There was a special glint in Joanna's gray-green eyes that spelled trouble. Ten minutes later, when she finished a phone call that would change her life, the glint had turned into a dazzling sparkle.

"Joanna, are you crazy?"

"Hold it, Gary. I've been asked that question all morning by everyone from the chief down to the file clerk. Don't you ask me, too."

"Then it's true. You really did ask Johnson for a one-year leave of absence."

"I really did, and he really said no. All he could guarantee was that there would be a spot for me somewhere in the agency when I returned. If I returned, of course."

"If? Joanna, have I told you about the shrink I saw a few years ago when I was feeling—"

"Gary, will you answer me one question honestly? No, wait. First, let me point out a few things: I am single, responsible to no one but myself; I am young, healthy, and unendingly competent; I just paid off my MasterCard account and now owe nobody anything; I have been breaking my neck trying to get ahead for ten years, and I find the place I'm heading a gross disappointment. So I ask you: What do I have to lose? Why should I listen to everybody telling me to be practical? Why should I have to be practical anyway? Give me one good reason, Gary." She stood at her desk, hands on hips, her eyes daring him to come up with a reply.

He couldn't. Instead, he gazed at her with awe and admiration. "You know something, babe: If anyone can pull this off, I do believe it's you. You've got guts, Jo."

She smiled, relief flooding over her features. "Thanks, Gary. But it isn't guts. I think desperation would be a better word. No, I'm not being fair to myself. This is going to be a true adventure—of the body and the spirit. Did I ever tell you about my great-grandmother who went from the wealthy comforts of upper-crust Philadelphia to the pioneering life in the wilds of Utah?"

"And there's also the uncle with the chicken farm. You obviously have adventure in your blood," he said, chuckling.

Joanna laughed, too, but when she spoke, her

tone was serious. "I think those pioneers discovered things we high-rise apartment dwellers have lost sight of. We pay for all the ease and conveniences of our lives by having to keep up a mad, insane pace, not to mention the earnings we need to maintain it all. There is something to be said for the simple life. I have enough capital now to stake myself for a year in which to capture that pioneering spirit, to find solace in accomplishments that have nothing to do with selling more perfume or toilet paper. Who knows? Maybe in the midst of all that tranquillity I'll even figure out what I really want out of life."

"Jo, I admire you. Maybe Julie and I will come up and visit once you're settled. Leave your phone number so I can at least call and tell you all about what you're not missing."

"No phone."

"No phone? That's not country; that's positively primitive."

"Yup, as they say in Vermont. Or some facsimile of that. Actually I think it's something more like 'Yahup.' I'll have to practice. Stop looking at me again as if I were crazy. You just said you admire me. I probably will get a phone put in— after a few months. But first I want to experience solitude in its pure form: no visits, no calls, no letters about all the sales I'm missing at Saks or Bonwit's. The first couple of months are going to be rough, so I figure if I'm forced to rely completely on myself, I'll be all the stronger for it once the winter sets in and I'm snowbound in the wilderness."

"I don't think I like the idea of your being alone in some wasteland."

"I'm exaggerating. There are some farms around. In desperation I could always ask for help. But I don't want to. That's the point. I want to do this on my own, or else I won't be able to consider myself an honorary pioneer." She grinned, squeezing Gary's shoulder. "So don't come up there rescuing me unless I send a smoke signal. Okay?"

"I'll be keeping my eye out for any suspicious puffs."

Gary ended up wishing her luck, offering to help her pack. But she was subletting her apartment intact since the cabin came furnished, so there would not be much to pack—"just the basics."

"Ayhup, nice little place you bought yourself, Miss Winfield."

Joanna stared at the old farmer, whose wizened face had a leathery look from decades of working outdoors. He was right in saying "little," she thought, wondering how the place had managed to shrink in a few short months. And "nice"—well, that depended on whether you liked early primitive architecture and decor. Ancient primitive, she corrected herself. For some reason her summer week up here, with the birds chirping, the bright sun shining, the rolling meadows abounding with buttercups had given the cabin and its furniture—what there was of it—a kind of rustic appeal. Right now it merely looked rustic.

Determined not to let her spirits drop after five minutes of country life, she walked over to the window and drew the gingham curtains. The curtains would do—especially after a good wash. She tried not to think about the fact that she planned to do her washing by hand rather than cart it to the town Laundromat twenty minutes down the road. That would be cheating according to her survival plan. Her great-grandmother hadn't had the option of a spin cycle.

Once she gazed out the window, she remembered why she had come up here. The area was beautiful—even more so than during the summer, now that autumn was slowly coloring the hills and forests. The sense of tranquillity was everywhere. Joanna turned back to face the room, deciding the furniture was perfectly serviceable, and she smiled at Chuck Harvey.

"It's going to be great," she said enthusiastically.

"This here's the only key to the place," he said, handing her a large old iron artifact. "Truth is, don't know that it locks anything. Ain't never known anyone to try. Not much here to steal, if you know what I mean." He had himself a good laugh over that while Joanna tried a smile. Being reminded of the lack of creature luxuries was not what she needed at this moment.

After old Mr. Harvey had left, Joanna felt better. She unpacked her suitcase, neatly folding her assortment of shirts and sweaters into the rickety chest of drawers and draping her jeans and corduroys over wire hangers in the closet. She quickly discovered the closet door did not shut properly, so she swung it open and closed a few times, then bent down to get a better view of the problem. Smiling to herself as she saw what was causing the difficulty, Joanna decided to set immediately to work. She opened a cumbersome wooden box which, besides her suitcase and a large carton of books and sketch pads, was all she had brought with her, and pulled out a brand-new saw. The box was filled with every tool she and the salesman at the hardware store could come up with—except those that had looked positively deadly.

She started back to the small bedroom and then remembered the hammer. After grabbing it, she walked with a jaunty step back to the closet door. Getting the door off its hinges was not easy, so Joanna felt a true rush of accomplishment when she finally got it disconnected and outside. After returning to her survival box for the portable sawhorses, she set them up in front of the house, placed the heavy wooden door on them, and began sawing away at the bottom edge.

"You need a plane."

Joanna looked up, startled. She hadn't heard anyone approach. But then these grounds weren't made of concrete echoing every step. The man was dark-haired, maybe in his mid-thirties, tall, with a complexion that had begun to weather, and on him the effect was ruggedly attractive. Joanna assumed from his well-worn jeans and often-washed work shirt that he must be one of the farmhands from the large dairy down the road.

"I'm not going anywhere," she said with a shrug, continuing to saw the door.

"You're what? Oh. That's not the kind of plane I meant." He laughed.

"It was a joke." Joanna watched his smile disappear. "I guess you didn't get it." She was irritated that he had been quick to assume she didn't know what she was doing—even if she didn't. She did own a newly purchased plane; the salesman had said it might come in handy. The only problem was that she had forgotten to ask him what it would come in handy for.

"You want some help with that?" he asked. His irritation at her snappy comeback seemed to have evaporated.

"No, thanks. I'm doing fine."

"Just being neighborly," he said lightly, making no effort to leave.

The saw slipped, missing Joanna's knee by a fraction of an inch.

"You have to be careful of the teeth. Could rip right through those designer jeans of yours. Be a pity—might cut your leg."

Joanna set the saw down. "If it makes you feel better, these are last year's designer jeans. And I am watching my leg and the saw's teeth. Now if you wouldn't mind *not* watching, I think I will do just fine."

"You don't take too well to advice, do you?" he said nonchalantly, and her strikingly attractive face grew hotly angry. He laughed. "That was a joke."

Joanna started to say something, then stopped herself. She gave him an assessing glance. This was no simple country boy, she decided. He was shrewder than she had imagined. She met his gaze. He was still smiling.

She smiled back. "Sorry. I'm not being very neighborly. I'm Joanna Winfield. I just bought this place. In fact, today's my first day here. I may look as if I don't know what I'm doing; that's because I don't. Not exactly anyway. But I chose to adopt this life-style so that I could learn by doing. And although I appreciate your offer of help, my only interest at this time is in helping myself. So it's nice to meet you, but I really would like to be left to my own mistakes. Don't take it as—"

"A brush-off?" He grinned.

"I wouldn't have put it quite that way." Joanna found his steady gaze disquieting.

"Well, that's the nice thing about country life. Folks up here pride themselves on being neighborly as well as on minding their own business. You might just find that both those qualities come in handy at times."

"Thanks, Mr. . . ."

"Sam Chase," he said as he started walking off. "I live down the road," he added, pausing to look back over his shoulder, "so if you find those mistakes you're learning from cause you any problems, stop by for some neighborly assistance." His look was not particularly neighborly at that moment.

He didn't wait for a reply. As he strode off, Joanna gave him one anyway.

"Don't hang around waiting for me to knock on your door, Mr. Chase. I learn fast."

Her parting shot would have been more effective if she hadn't screamed in pain as the door slipped off the sawhorses and onto her foot.

CHAPTER TWO

As soon as Sam lifted the door back onto the sawhorses, Joanna dropped to her knees, grasping her foot with a painful cry. There was no point in trying to save face at the risk of losing her instep.

Sam eased her down firmly onto the ground and without a word gently pulled off her sneaker and sock. Joanna was equally silent. *Well,* she decided, *at least I won't be putting my foot in my mouth for a while.*

"It's only a bruise," he said as Joanna flinched in pain under his ministrations.

"Only!" She grabbed her foot away to check it for herself. "It's all swollen. I've probably broken half a dozen bones."

"Not even one. Anyway, you should know better than to do heavy work with sneakers on. If you were wearing steel-tipped work boots, this would never have happened," he said pleasantly, watching her carefully tug her sock back on.

"Are all country folk so damn smug?" she muttered. "I should know better," she said

27

mimickingly as she got up, refusing Sam's help. Balancing her weight on her uninjured foot, she met his gaze. "How am I supposed to know about work boots—with steel tips no less. They aren't exactly *de rigueur* in New York City."

"You aren't in New York City," he pointed out with a smile, "although something tells me you might be on your way back in no time at all. Admen—pardon—women, don't—"

"How did you know I was in advertising?" she interrupted. She could guess the rest of his remark.

"Another aspect of country life, Miss Winfield, is that everybody knows what's happening with everyone else within a twenty-mile radius— often before a person knows it herself."

"I thought country folk minded their own business." She glanced sideways at him, deciding to forgo the additional pain of trying to replace her sneaker. Having gently eased her injured foot to the ground, she found that she could put some weight on it without screaming. *So, okay,* she said to herself, *maybe nothing is broken.*

"You do have a lot to learn." He smiled at the way she was tentatively testing the damage to her foot. "Gossip is one of the leading pastimes around these parts. Even now, at this very minute, I guarantee you word is spreading that the new lady from the city bashed her foot trying to saw up her door and Sam Chase came to her rescue."

Joanna grimaced, surreptitiously glancing

around just to make sure Sam Chase was teasing her.

He noticed and laughed. "I say, let's be brave and risk the gossip. I'll help you back into your house."

"Oh, no, thanks," Joanna replied. "Can't have a local boy's reputation ruined by some hussy from the city."

"Is that what you are? Hussy is a word that's passé even in these backwoods."

"You are an irritating man, Mr. Chase," Joanna said, carefully bending down to retrieve her sneaker. "I don't think we're going to have to worry about gossip because I don't intend to—"

"I've been told that before—"

"Oh, I believe that."

"But then again, after people get to know me better, they find I grow on them. Once you get used to me, I'm really kind of lovable." He wore a decidedly enigmatic smile as he spoke.

Joanna tried to ignore the huskiness of his voice, the sensual undertones of his words, the gorgeous rugged physique, and the way his warm brown eyes surveyed her. She reminded herself that she was not up here to find a man. Besides, she was pretty sure she didn't like Sam Chase. He was smug and opinionated, and he obviously saw her as some urban ding-a-ling who didn't know a plane from a screwdriver.

With haughty disdain she announced, "I really don't plan to find out whether you could grow on me or not."

29

His smile deepened, causing Joanna to bristle more. "I did not intend to make an enemy my first day here, Mr. Chase, so let's part amicably . . . and permanently. I came here for some tranquillity and relaxation, so thanks for your assistance, and good-bye." She turned brusquely and began to hobble off.

"What about your door?"

She glanced at him over her shoulder, then switched her gaze to the heavy door. There was no way she'd be able to drag the thing back into the house in her condition. And she was certainly never going to get it back on its hinges by herself. Returning her gaze to Sam, she felt slightly ridiculous and wholly adolescent. How had she given up ten years of maturity in one day? Nothing seemed to be working out the way she had fantasized.

Joanna still hadn't spoken when Sam finally said, "It's going to rain. The door is likely to warp if you leave it sitting outside."

She wanted to come up with a snappy rejoinder about knowing that wood warps when it's wet, but she stopped herself. The thought of feeling still more sophomoric didn't sit well.

"Would you mind helping me inside with it?"

"Be happy to."

At least his answer wasn't smug, Joanna thought gratefully. Maybe he was tired of the adolescent game, too.

Sam lifted the door easily and followed Joanna into the house.

"You can just lean it against the closet." She pointed to her bedroom.

He carried it into the room, replaced it on its hinges, and shoved it shut. The door still wouldn't close properly.

When he walked back into the living room, where Joanna sat on the couch, he said, "I'll bring over a plane and fix it for you tomorrow if you like."

"I have a plane." Her voice again had a biting edge, so she added more pleasantly, "I'm sure I'll be able to manage it."

Sam nodded. "You're bound and determined, are you?"

Joanna looked up sharply. She saw that his smile was warm and only slightly teasing.

"Yup. Bound and determined. I may look helpless and inept, Mr. Chase, but believe it or not, I am a strong, competent woman, and I really do learn quickly. Maybe you think I'm foolish, but I want to prove to myself that I can. . . . I told a friend back in the city that I wanted to be a pioneer like some of my ancestors. Really tough it out, experience what it's like to—to grow my own food, furnish my own heat, fix my own closet door"—she grinned—"with a plane, naturally."

"What was your friend's reaction?"

"He thought I was crazy, but he also admitted that he admired me."

"Well, I have to say I agree with your friend."

"About being crazy or admiring me?"

"Some of both," he said with a laugh. "I like

31

your spirit, Joanna. I also think you're an exceptionally beautiful woman—smashed-up foot and all."

"Get that look out of your eye, Sam Chase. I don't want to guess what your fantasies are about city women, but you had better know that I'm an expert at karate and I've had a lot of practice using it. I was not planning on needing it up here. I'm going to be too busy learning about survival to get caught up in—"

He cocked his head, his expression definitely smug now. "I only handed you a compliment, not a place in my bed. Slow down. I like to get to know a lady before I get serious."

"Oh, and is bedding a woman serious business to you?" Joanna flung back, determined not to let his retort intimidate her.

"Up in the country we take our romancing very seriously. There aren't that many gorgeous women to go around, so we have to select carefully."

"Pity," she said, "I'm not in the market for romance."

"That is a pity, but then again, you might change your mind. Women are known to do that."

"Not this woman, especially not if you throw out another one of those god-awful chauvinistic remarks."

"I had a feeling that one would get to you."

Joanna shook her head, propping her foot up on a pillow. The acute pain was turning into a slow but steady ache. "I'm beginning to feel confident that we bring out the worst in each other."

"Maybe we're not trying hard enough," Sam suggested, watching Joanna struggle to find a comfortable position for her foot. "It will feel better tomorrow, but a couple of aspirin might help for now."

"No. No aspirin," Joanna answered with determination. "I threw out all my bottles of aspirin, antacids, antihistamines, and everything else I used to get myself through my days at Bailey and Johnson. I'm not going to need that junk up here." Her voice cracked. Some pioneer —floored the first day by her own closet door. She was hungry and tired, her foot was killing her, and the wonderful brisk air she'd been anticipating now felt disappointingly damp and cold. Her wood stove presented yet another challenge. She had been so damn confident this morning she'd neglected to ask old Harvey how to operate the dumb thing. A sinking depression was fast taking all the pioneering spirit out of her.

Sam bent down beside her and lifted her chin toward him. "It isn't all that tough up here," he murmured. "You'll get the hang of it."

"Oh, yeah," she responded, blinking away a traitorous tear.

"Yeah." He bent closer, his hand still cupping her chin, and lightly kissed her lips.

"Why did you do that?" she asked, eyeing him warily.

"I prefer to see you mad rather than miserable." He looked down at her, his palm skimming her neck before he released her.

"It didn't work."

"Let's try again."

She laughed then. "I must be crazy."

"I thought we'd already decided that." Sam was ready for another go.

She turned her head to the side so that his lips landed on her neck. He made the most of the switch.

"Please, Sam. Honest. I'm really feeling kind of dizzy."

He stopped and looked at her. She was pale. With a rapid grasp of her shoulders he sat her up abruptly and pushed her head down to her lap in the process.

"Take deep breaths."

"I feel ridiculous," she said between breaths.

"I feel flattered." He continued to exert a light pressure on her back, preventing her from sitting straight up.

"Shut up," she growled after her next inhalation. "It's my injury, not your little seduction that's gone to my head."

"If that's what you want to think . . ."

"Will you let go of me, damn it? I'm not dizzy anymore."

"See. I knew if I could get you angry, you'd feel better."

"Oh, God, how did I get myself into this predicament?" She moaned, grabbing an afghan off the back of the couch and wrapping it around her shoulders. "If you're going to hang around, will you make yourself useful and go start that ancient monstrosity over there?"

"Now I don't rightly know if I should. What was that speech of yours about being so all-fired determined to do everything yourself?"

"I'll start tomorrow." She was just too cold and miserable to argue.

"Fair enough." Instead of heading toward the stove, however, he stood and lifted her up in his arms.

"What the hell are you doing now?" she cried, stunned at finding herself so easily levitated.

"It's going to be just as cold tomorrow afternoon, so you'd better watch and learn how to get this monster roaring. You do learn quickly, right?"

Again she couldn't argue, this time because she was too shaken by the way it felt to be cradled against his broad chest. She even began thinking about what a second kiss might feel like.

She forgot the fantasy when he dropped her rather unceremoniously on the floor beside the stove.

"Do you mind being careful about how you dump me," she snapped.

"Sorry. I wasn't meaning to dump you. Have to be a fool to do something like that when we're just beginning to get acquainted."

"You were wrong before, Sam. To know you is not to love you."

"I'll settle for less." Before she could counter-attack, he demanded, "Now pay attention, or when winter rolls around, you'll be a beautiful bundle of goose bumps." With expert ease he placed crumpled newspaper, kindling, and a couple of small logs in the stove, set the dampers on their maximum opening, lit the fire with one match, and shut the door.

"It looks easy enough," she observed.

"The trick is in learning how to adjust the dampers. If you leave them open too long, your wood will go up in smoke mighty fast. If you lower them too quickly, the fire will go out and you'll have to start all over again."

"Okay."

"Wait till you've got a real good blast, and then close them nice and slow."

"Okay."

"Give it about twenty minutes—"

"I really think I can handle it, Sam. Thanks for the lesson."

"Think you'll be ready for a test tomorrow night?"

"Very slick, Mr. Chase. But I'm not interested in tests—written or oral. Get the message?"

"Okay." He shrugged. Reaching down, he took Joanna's hand, shook it firmly, and said, "Nice meeting you. Best of luck. Oh, and by the way, you've got a real talent for kissing. I hope you're as skilled in all things, Miss Winfield."

The next moment he was gone, leaving Joanna staring openmouthed at the front door.

Chuck Harvey had not gotten around to installing that indoor shower. The thought of stepping outside into the cold downpour and hobbling to the outdoor shower she had so adored last summer was not something Joanna would even consider at this point. Having just finished a meager meal of chicken noodle soup and a dry grilled cheese sandwich—Mr. Harvey had forgotten the butter on the list she'd read him over the phone from New York—she decided her large, modern inside bathtub back home was the most wonderful object she'd ever owned. She settled for a bucket of hot water into which she stuck her aching foot. It was turning a richly colored black and blue, but the swelling had gone down considerably. Sam had known what he was talking about when he'd assured her there were no broken bones.

Joanna was not surprised that Sam Chase had popped into her thoughts. She realized now that she had not found out a thing about the man. She had no idea who he was, where he lived, what he did for a living. So far, beyond admitting that he was very attractive and obviously bright, the only thing she had going with Farmer Brown here was a well-matched juvenile repartee.

Of course, the fire in the stove went out. She had shut the damn dampers too quickly. She reminded herself that she was postponing her fight for independence until tomorrow, grabbed every blanket she could find in the cabin, and buried herself beneath them in bed. As long as she didn't lift her hands out of the covers, she was warm enough. She went to sleep that night wishing for Indian summer.

Her wish didn't come true. But it had stopped raining. A misty fog was still clinging to the ground when Joanna got up the courage to remove the warm blankets and get out of bed.

Sam had been right. Her foot did feel better today. She frowned, though, annoyed that thoughts of Sam had cropped up first thing this morning.

She set about planning her day. Besides fixing her closet door with that plane, stocking her kitchen with something other than soup, and bringing more firewood into the house, her biggest order of the day was to put Sam Chase firmly out of her mind.

By the early afternoon she had accomplished most of what she'd set out to do. She'd made a run into town and shopped at the local general store for provisions, chatting with Mr. Kelsey, the proprietor, about the awful weather they'd been having. Once home Joanna carried more than twenty armfuls of wood into the living room, where she stacked them neatly onto a wrought iron holder, and she even got her door planed and back in place. It now closed with beautiful ease. Exhausted, Joanna lay down on her bed and surveyed her handiwork with pride. The nifty little plane lay beside her. She picked it up and laughed. Sam's opening line from yesterday came back to her.

So much for getting the man firmly out of her

mind. She heard a sound outside her window. After bolting out of bed, she smoothed her hair, took a few deep breaths, and strolled nonchalantly outside.

"Hi."

Joanna swallowed a small flash of disappointment. The visitor was not Sam. "Hi."

A girl, maybe thirteen or fourteen—Joanna wasn't good at guessing the age of kids—dressed in blue jeans and a plaid cowboy shirt, her hair in slightly mussed braids, stood looking at Joanna with a curious stare.

"Do you live around here?" Joanna asked cordially.

The girl nodded in a northerly direction.

"Go to school nearby?"

This time she nodded southward.

Joanna shifted her weight. Her experience in conversations with adolescents was limited. And this girl was not being particularly cooperative.

"Well, uh, nice meeting you. I'd better get back to my, uh, work." Joanna turned to leave.

"Sam told me you come from New York City. Ever been to the Statue of Liberty? I just heard the other day that the whole thing might collapse."

Joanna's ears perked up at the mention of Sam. "Um, Statue of Liberty, no. I've never been there actually."

"That's weird."

Joanna laughed. "No, not really. It's typical that many residents of a place don't visit the sites tourists see all the time. One of these days I should go out there, though."

"You going back to live in New York?"

"I don't know. I just got here. Figure I might as well try this for a while." She laughed, realizing she was even beginning to talk like the locals. Still needed to add a good "ayhup," though. She'd have to remember that for next time.

"It's nice up here. But it's kind of dull. No action," the girl said with a remarkably sophisticated air.

"No action?"

"Yeah. Sam says you'll go crazy up here 'cause there isn't any action like there is in New York. Actually I wasn't sure exactly what he meant by 'action.' But Sam's like that. Says things sometimes and just figures I understand what he means, so I go along with him. Usually I end up figuring it out."

"You're very smart then," Joanna said, glad the girl was verbal after all. She wondered just what her connection was to Sam, but something held her back from asking.

"Sure I'm smart. Sam says I'm probably going to go to Harvard or Yale or some college like that. Me, I'm planning to go to the University of Vermont—if I go to college, that is. Keep it to yourself, though. Sam would get upset if he knew what I was thinking."

"You still have some time to decide anyway."

"True. But I'm the kind of person that once I make up my mind, I pretty much keep to what I've decided."

Joanna had to envy her. If only she had such confidence. "What's your name?"

"That's another of the problems Sam and I have. Don't get me wrong. We get along real well, Sam and I. There are just a few sticky issues that cause problems. My name's Penelope. Now I ask you, would you want to go around being called Penelope?" She gave Joanna a challenging stare.

Joanna shook her head no. "You like Penny?"

"Ugh, no." She grimaced so vehemently that Joanna had to laugh. "Penny? God, how could anybody want to be called Penny? That's worse than Penelope. Penny, nickel, dime—I suffered through six years of grade school with those dumb jokes."

"I see what you mean," Joanna said with a smile of understanding.

"Until I turn sixteen, I'm stuck with Penelope. Sam says when I'm sixteen, I can change it legally if I still hate it. I'm considering Jane. It's simple, to the point, and there aren't too many bad nicknames for it. Oh, there's Plain Jane, but I wouldn't mind that one. Nothing wrong with being plain. Sam says I'm going to grow into my natural beauty. That's another little issue between us, but I don't argue with him over it, even though, between you and me, I think he's full of baloney. He thinks I mind that I'm not going to turn into some glamour puss, but I really don't want to be noticed for my outer beauty."

"Very wise."

"Yeah, you've got that problem, huh? Sam said you were really gorgeous, and except when it comes to me, he's not quick to dish out compliments. He's real fussy."

"I'm sure of that," Joanna said.

"You like Sam? I think he's the best-looking man in all of Brandon, maybe all of Vermont. He could be in movies, I bet. He's got oodles of sex appeal."

"How old are you, Penelope?"

"Fifteen. Less than seven months till Sweet Sixteen. And very mature and sophisticated for my age." She grinned. "Sam's been telling me that ever since I can remember. His favorite line is to say I was born twenty-five."

"You must know Sam very well."

"Of course I do. He's my father."

Joanna had already figured this out. She'd merely been seeking confirmation.

"What does your mother say about your father's observations?" Joanna asked with a nonchalance that did not come easily.

"Well, she doesn't say much."

"Oh." No doubt Sam would get around to telling her that his wife didn't understand him. She, however, was not planning to give him the opportunity.

"My mom's been dead since I was two," Penelope added as she swung her backpack into place. "Oh, Sam says to tell you he hopes your foot is feeling better. Is it?"

"Uh, better?" A slow smile curved her lips. "Yes. Tell him it's much better."

"I'll tell him. Oh, by the way, do I call you Joanna?"

"My friends call me Jo."

Penelope nodded. "Jo . . . yeah, I like that. See you around, Jo."

"See you, Penelope." They both grinned.

CHAPTER THREE

When the water heater first went on the fritz, Joanna handled the situation admirably. She took her trusty screwdriver in hand, undid and then tightened every screw she could find, fiddled with the connectors, and, as a final touch, gave the workings one good hammer swat. The tap water spurted out first lukewarm and then steamy hot.

Her sense of accomplishment lasted for two days. The second time the heater gave out, none of her tried and true efforts worked. She ended up trudging the mile into town to the local hardware store in the hope of finding someone to fix it.

Dennis Butler, a wiry little man, stopped by three chilly days later, took one look at the archaic heater, and told her it had seen its last day.

"What do I do now?" she asked, resigned to the heater's untimely (at least by her schedule) demise.

"You'll have to order one through the Sears catalogue. Unless you want to boil your water on the stove. Still, some folks get by that way," Dennis said laconically.

Joanna decided her pioneering spirit did not extend that far. A little automatic hot water was one luxury she wasn't ready to forfeit. Besides, her plan to have that indoor shower installed did not include rigging up pots of boiled water overhead.

When she found out what a new water heater would cost, Joanna almost reconsidered her need for modest comforts. Then she mentally compared nice steamy showers to the arduous sponge baths she'd gone through before crawling into her chilly bed each night, and she marched down to the Sears store to order the heater. She would do without something else instead, she decided as she calculated the dwindling balance in her checking account. And she had thought country living would be cheap!

Four days later Dennis Butler installed the new heater while Joanna made them both some coffee. He was her first visitor in more than two weeks. She was lonely. Solitude had its up side after years of constant intense interactions, but it had its down side, too. Joanna was discovering she had some basic needs for socializing, and she'd found herself hoping more than once that Sam Chase or Penelope would stop by for a visit. She hadn't seen either of them since she'd first moved in. Chastising herself for not having been very neighborly, she decided she would make an effort to be more cordial if she had another opportunity.

She brought the coffee over to Dennis, who was just finishing up.

"Think that should do you," he said, fastening the last screw. "Might cost you a bit more to run. This one is bigger than the one you had in here before."

"I was hoping to save money because this heater should be more efficient," Joanna countered with logic.

"Yeah. That's what they tell ya. You try explaining that to the electric company when your bills come in. No way around it. You put in a bigger heater, you're heating up more water, you're using up more electricity, no matter how efficiently. Logic—plain and simple." Dennis took his coffee and swallowed a large gulp.

Joanna had a depressing feeling that Dennis's homespun logic was probably more accurate than hers. She felt even worse when she asked him what he would charge to install a shower now that she had reliable hot water.

"That shouldn't be too much of a problem," he said at first as he checked out the space and the existent bathroom plumbing. "Of course, we've got to figure in the cost of the stall, the new pipes, the fixtures. . . . I could probably keep it under a thousand. If we don't run into problems. Once we start messing around with the old pipes, we just might find we need to replace them, too. Then we're talking more time, and more time means—"

"More money," Joanna finished with her newly acquired realization that everything cost

46

at least double what she had estimated in her fantasies. She was fast ridding herself of dreamy, romantic notions of carefree and relatively cost-free country living.

Dennis walked over to the kitchen and deposited his empty mug in the sink. "No hurry about letting me know if you want to go ahead on the shower. This time of year business is slow." He looked around at the living room. "You sure have fixed the place up nice. Real cozy."

Joanna smiled. It was true. Washing all the curtains, adding an inexpensive throw over the worn couch, sparking up the kitchen table with colorful woven mats, and hanging a few prints and posters on the walls had turned the rather bleak cabin into a small but charming little home. Her spirits lifted. Money might be going out faster than she had hoped, but over the past few weeks she had acquired some new and valuable skills for survival. Not only could she now light her wood stove with one match, but she had gathered a barrelful of kindling from the woods, chopped up three downed logs on her property to perfect stove size, and even built herself a cart to lug the heavy logs from her neatly stacked woodpile to the cabin.

Her handiwork on the closet door had been so successful that she'd tackled her bureau drawers and kitchen cabinets as well. Not everything worked perfectly, but Joanna was proud of her growing skills in carpentry.

If she could be a carpenter, why not a plumber? she thought with a determined glint in her eye. Surely it would cost her half what she would pay Dennis. Her time, fortunately, was free.

"Do you think I could figure out how to install that shower myself?" she asked Dennis as he was starting for the door.

He turned around and gave her an appraising look. "You ever done any plumbing?"

"Well . . . not exactly. But I'm pretty handy," she responded with less than enthusiastic confidence.

"I'm not pushing for the business, mind you," he said, "but I'd say leave it to someone who knows how to mess with that stuff. Now, if there aren't any surprises along the way, I guess you could do it."

"Maybe I'll be lucky," she said. "Back in New York I always used to see ads on TV for all those how-to books that teach you everything—from building your own deck to fixing leaky toilets. I just might pick up a 'how to put in a shower' book, follow the easy one-, two-, three-step illustrated guide and keep myself solvent for another month or two."

Dennis shrugged. "Well, you know where to reach me if you change your mind. I don't go in much for learning by books myself. Those easy steps aren't always as easy as they seem."

Joanna handed Dennis his money for installing the water heater. Watching yet another large sum slip away made her even more determined to do the shower herself. She wasn't ignoring Dennis's warnings so much as convincing herself she would be extracautious and diligent.

The first step was to find the book. She had already visited the tiny one-room library in town, and although its collection of current novels was sadly lacking, she had a feeling books on plumbing would be easier to come by.

Joanna realized, as she applied some lipstick and blush before she left for the library, that she wanted to look presentable if she ran into Sam in town. She even admitted her hope she would run into him. Since their initial meeting her irritation had given way to curiosity and a little more than casual interest. In her past visits to the town she had the opportunity to see, if not actually meet, most of the people who lived in Brandon. She had to agree with Penelope. Sam Chase was probably the best-looking man in town. She wasn't ready to go so far as giving him a hands-down vote for the whole state, but she had no doubt he would at least make runner-up.

Her admission of interest in Sam Chase was a case of honesty winning out over common sense. However, she still chose to construe that interest in purely platonic terms. Sam did have a certain charm and wit. And for more than two weeks Joanna had hardly talked to a soul beyond a few comments about the weather with local shopkeepers or discussions about water heaters and showers with the town handyman. Even some flirtatious repartee was beginning to have its appeal.

Joanna was still somewhat of an attraction in the town. Everyone knew her as the city lady who had bought the old Harvey cabin. Foolishly bought it, Joanna gathered from the looks she received from the townsfolk. Everyone was relatively cordial, but Joanna clearly got the message that she was an outsider in a way she never felt among the thousands of strangers surrounding her every day in New York City. There everyone was a bit of an alien. Here everyone belonged by virtue of birth or thirty or more years of settling—everyone but her and maybe a handful of other relative newcomers to town. Brandon was not experiencing a population explosion, to say the least.

She had as much difficulty relating to the locals as they did to her. Once she'd finished chatting about the weather or the raccoon she'd seen in her backyard the other day, she ran out of steam.

When she was in town among people, she found the sense of loneliness harder to cope with than when she was by herself at her cabin. Every time she wandered in and out of the few stores lining Main Street she had to fight off her nagging doubts about lasting through a full year of country life. Her strength lay in her determination to come out of this experience a winner. Exactly what she would win was no longer as clear as it had been in her fantasies, but she had never liked the taste of failure . . . of any kind. The drive to succeed, to win, had been her biggest asset at the ad agency, and she intended to use that talent to keep her pioneering spirit alive . . . and fighting.

She was right about the library's having just the book she needed. There were more than three easy steps to installing the shower, but none of the steps seemed terribly complex. All she needed to do was get someone to translate half the terminology for her. Galvanized plumbing versus copper plumbing, stop valves, compression faucets, and C-clamps—these things had not come up in any of her day-to-day conversations in Manhattan.

Bob Webster, who ran the small hardware store in town, was not particularly helpful. First of all, he informed her, he would have to special order most of what she needed, and second of all, he had already spoken to Dennis Butler. They agreed that the little lady from the city was biting off more than she could handle.

"I've already read half the book," she argued, "and it seems simple enough. Once I see what the actual parts look like and understand exactly what the purpose of each one is, I'm sure I'll have no difficulty putting them together."

"You're going to need a divertor mechanism for your project, but you probably figured that out already from your book."

Joanna swung around at the sound of Sam Chase's deep voice.

"Hi there, neighbor," he greeted her. "Don't worry about Miss Winfield having trouble with that shower, Bob. She's a fast learner."

She did not appreciate Sam's little innuendo,

nor did she like Bob's broad grin. However, right now understanding how to install her shower was more important to Joanna than preserving her pride.

"Since you know about divertors, maybe you know about ball and cam mechanisms and whether they're preferable to a self-contained cartridge faucet." Joanna flipped to the page in the book describing faucet options.

Sam glanced at the page and then gave her an amused look. "Seems like it's all there in black and white. I wouldn't want to spoil . . . the excitement of discovery for you by trying to butt in. I seem to remember your saying you were up here to learn by doing. I kind of felt a little hurt at the time, but now I have to admit I do admire your determination to manage without unwanted intrusions." He turned to Bob. "Did that dehumidifier come in yet?"·

"Got it in this morning's shipment. If you want to come back in another hour or so, I'll have it ready for you."

Sam nodded and walked over to a wall display of door hinges. He pulled off two of them and set them on the counter. "Add those to the bill. I'll go pick up my mail and be back later."

Joanna was adept at giving brush-offs, but her experience in being on the receiving end of them was nil. Until this afternoon. She not only didn't like it but had no intention of accepting it. She followed Sam through the door, calling out to him. He stopped and turned to face her.

"Just what was all that talk about folks up here

being neighborly?" she sputtered. "I see right through you, Sam Chase. So you thought you'd give me a little taste of my own medicine. And here I was, for the past two weeks, hoping I'd run into you so I could apologize for—for . . . Oh, forget it." She finished in frustration.

"I'm sorry," he said, grabbing hold of her arm as she turned away in anger. "I guess I *was* dishing out a little of what I sampled that day."

"You should be sorry," she snapped, lowering her voice as an elderly woman walked by and greeted Sam with a curious smile.

"Going to get your mail?" He still held onto her elbow.

Joanna hesitated.

"Maybe I can tell you about faucets along the way," he said with a friendly grin. "I did apologize. Now are we going to start a new battle so soon, Jo?" He laughed at her cautious glance. "Jo is the name you go by with friends, isn't it?"

"I don't think we've gotten off to a great start for a budding friendship. I'm not even sure we could be friends."

"I don't see why not. We seem to have a lot in common."

"We do?" Joanna gave him a skeptical look.

"Sure. We both can be smug and self-righteous on occasion. We're also determined, stubborn, too quick to take offense, and fast learners. Another thing: Neither of us likes being given the brush-off."

Joanna grinned. "You seem to have me

pegged. That makes me a little uneasy," she admitted, her smile fading.

Sam eyed her with open warmth. "We also share honesty in common. Besides the fact that you're very beautiful, it's your most winning asset."

"Is that my cue to say it's yours, too?"

"Honesty is something I value highly in myself and in those I care about. It's also a trait that frequently gets me in hot water."

"I'm not surprised."

"I have a feeling that with you in town I might be stepping into hot water again. Truth is, you've been on my mind quite a lot these past few weeks. I've been trying to build up my courage to risk another brush-off."

"You wouldn't have gotten it," Joanna said truthfully. "Don't get me wrong, Sam," she hurried to add, "I'm interested only in being more neighborly. I still intend to stick with my self-survival plan."

"You sure you want to talk faucets then?" he asked lightly.

They walked together to the post office, and for the first time Joanna felt like a part of the community as the two of them smiled and greeted some of the local people passing by.

She'd received a few letters from friends and a flyer from Bloomingdale's advertising a new perfume. She started to toss the sealed packet into the trash, but Sam stopped her. Having taken it from her hands, he opened it and sniffed the scent.

"Pretty nice," he commented, "but I prefer yours." He smiled warmly as he looked in her eyes.

Joanna returned his smile, but she had an abrupt sense of having taken her own step into hot water. This was not the kind of hot water she was hoping for.

"Let's stick to faucets, not perfumes." They both noticed the small catch in her voice.

"I'll tell you about them over lunch."

"Since this is a consultation of sorts, it will be my treat," Joanna insisted, trying to cool things off with a businesslike attitude.

"You sure know how to take charge. You must have been a terrific ad exec."

"I was. I intend to become a terrific plumber as well. Where do we eat?"

"Well, Sardi's and Elaine's are a bit off the beaten path up here, so let's go to the Pine Tree Inn. It's the most lavish place in town, and since it's your treat, I might as well milk this consultation for all it's worth."

"If that's the case, I might have to get some advice on valves as well as faucets," Joanna said teasingly.

"You know, I've done a bit of plumbing in my day. I could give you a helping hand."

"I'm in the market only for advice, thanks."

Sam got the message. It was probably just as well that they didn't get too friendly, he told himself. Joanna Winfield might have some traits in common with him, but she was also worlds removed from his small patch of earth—a patch

55

he happened to love and cherish. Joanna was tough and determined, but she was also ninety-nine percent city. He smiled to himself thinking about the fable of the country mouse and the city mouse. In the end they both went their separate ways, appreciating their life-styles and environments. No, it wouldn't do to foster this attraction to a woman who probably still carried subway tokens in her purse.

So why had he suggested lunch? Sam asked himself as he led her down the street to the inn. He pushed the question aside as she caught hold of his arm.

"Am I dressed all right to go in there?"

He looked down at the form-fitting turtleneck sweater under her open Windbreaker, then at the pair of last year's designer jeans accentuating her slender waist and long legs, and he grinned.

"You look just fine."

Gazing at her appreciatively, he knew exactly why he had suggested lunch. Now all he had to do was come up with a different fable—one that had a happier ending.

The waitress greeted Sam by name and asked how his daughter was doing.

"She's a handful, as always," Sam assured her. "This year she's going in for downhill racing and wants a pair of Solomon ski boots."

"Want to wager she'll get them in the end?" The waitress smiled, apparently certain she'd be the winner of that bet.

"She's begrudgingly taken on a few more

chores to try to save up for them. I admit I agreed to match her half if she keeps up the good work—and doesn't let her grades fall." Sam picked up the menu. "What do you recommend today, Carol? The beef stew or the turkey pot pie?"

"George made up the turkey this morning. Go with that."

"Sounds good to me. How about you, Jo?"

"I'll have a BLT and a large glass of milk, thanks." Joanna caught the surreptitious glance Carol gave Sam before she turned away.

"Is there something wrong with bacon, lettuce, and tomato?" Joanna asked, puzzled by the waitress's reaction.

"Around here, when you ask for advice, people expect you'll take it. In this case, Carol also happens to be the cook's wife, so I think she took your rejection of the turkey a little personally."

"I wasn't the one who asked for advice about what to order," she pointed out.

"Well, that's another thing about life in the country. Carol took it for granted I was speaking for both of us."

"So I noticed." The logic that worked for her in New York City seemed to be failing her on a regular basis in Brandon.

"You'll get used to it." He grinned, certain that was not the response she wanted.

"I don't intend to." Joanna returned the grin. "I moved up here to be a pioneer, not a second-class citizen."

"Tell me something, Jo. Why would a smart,

sophisticated, successful woman trade in her high-paying, high-powered career to learn plumbing in a town that is this foreign to her? Are you running away from a broken romance or a lousy marriage or something?"

"Let's just say 'or something.' It's a long story, and with your not being a part of it, I doubt you'd understand." Joanna glanced up at Carol and smiled as the woman deposited her BLT on the scalloped white paper place mat. Carol did not smile back, but Joanna doubted she would have smiled even if she'd ordered the turkey.

"Does that mean there are no broken romances?" Sam persisted, unperturbed by her effort to drop the topic.

"I'm not suffering from a broken heart, Sam, nor did I leave some poor guy with one in New York."

"If it isn't romance that drove you up here . . ."

"Nothing drove me. No, I guess that's not true. In a way a guy did give me a good shove in this direction." She eyed him squarely. "His name's Cinderfella. Once we were finished with each other, I knew the time had come for me to get out of his life for—for a while anyway."

"So that was your brainchild," he commented.

"You saw it?"

"Don't look so surprised. We read magazines up here just like folks in the cities." He had to laugh as he spotted the flush in her cheeks.

"Well, I just thought you probably read things like *Country Life* or *Yankee* or—"

"Or *The Farmer's Almanac?*" He chuckled. "I read those, too. And I have to admit Penelope is the one who's always buying *Cosmopolitan, Redbook,* and *People.* I just sneak a peek at them once in a while for diversion. The Cinderfella ad is in every one of those magazines. It isn't the kind of spread that goes unnoticed."

"It had better not. It's the best thing I did for Bailey and Johnson. And that ad provided work for twenty of the most beautiful models in New York."

"I'll attest to that," he said with playfully exaggerated enthusiasm. "So tell me more about old Cinder. How come he drove you here to Brandon? You sound mighty proud of your accomplishment."

"Pride has little to do with sanity sometimes. I found after spending twenty-three and a half hours a day, day after day after day, on that ad that my sanity was wearing thin. And my imaginary ulcer was getting too real for comfort. I needed a change."

"You always resort to such drastic measures?" He studied her with open curiosity.

"Not always. I have to admit I wasn't altogether prepared for how drastic the change was going to be. But," she added, the glint of determination returning to her gray-green eyes, "it's a terrific challenge."

"Something else we share in common. I love a good challenge, too."

Joanna looked at Sam's broad smile and then studied her half-eaten sandwich. Her challenge right now was to finish this lunch while trying to defuse the charge traveling between her and Sam. A snappy comeback at this moment would only add to the problem, so she concentrated on her BLT.

Sam tried equally hard to focus on his turkey pot pie. It wasn't like him at all to be so persistently flirtatious. Sure, he'd been teasingly flippant with an attractive woman on occasion, but this was different. He wasn't really teasing with Joanna. And each time he chastised himself for pursuing an interest that was obviously pointless, he found himself saying something more provocative than the last time.

Both of them forgot about the unanswered plumbing questions until the bill came. Joanna reached for it, but Sam stopped her, his hand resting on hers.

"I didn't earn that meal," he pointed out. "I guess we'll have to reschedule the consultation. How about dinner tonight over at my place?"

Joanna hesitated. Those charges were even stronger with actual contact, so she edged her hand out from under his. She knew the wisest course would be to turn down his invitation and return to her earlier aloof stance. On the other hand, she'd already had two weeks of dining alone and listening to staticky music on her radio.

"Penelope would get a kick out of talking with you again," Sam said softly. "She was quite taken with her new friend, Jo. In fact, I've had to remind her on several occasions not to go bothering you over at your place."

"I've been hoping she'd come by again. I was pretty taken with her, too. She's welcome to drop over whenever she likes. Please let her know."

"How about telling her yourself tonight?"

Joanna smiled. "I'd like that."

They walked back over to Webster's hardware store, where Sam picked up his dehumidifier and Joanna told the clerk she'd stop by tomorrow to give her definite plumbing order.

"Can I give you a lift?" Sam offered.

"No, thanks. It might spoil me."

"Wouldn't want to do that." He started toward his car. "See you at my place . . . say, seven?"

"Where is your place?" she called out.

"Chase dairy farm. Two and a quarter miles down the road from your house. You won't miss it. It's a big spread. Penelope and I live in the white farmhouse thirty yards behind the wooden sign."

For a moment Joanna only took in the fact that this man who she thought was a poor local farmhand was actually the owner of a large dairy farm. When she realized there'd be a more-than-two-mile hike over to his house for dinner, he was already pulling out. He slowed down as he passed.

"I was going to offer to pick you up tonight, but now I'm beginning to understand your rugged independence. Very admirable. See you at seven."

He left her in a puff of dust, standing at the side of the road, muttering to herself.

CHAPTER FOUR

Joanna was not in a good mood when she finally arrived at Sam's house that evening. Several times during the forty-minute walk along the rough dirt road she almost turned back. Only her pride and the thought of another solitary meal kept her going. And of course, that consultation with Sam about her plumbing project. Her irritation and the cool evening air had encouraged a particularly brisk pace. Catching her breath, she now approached the front door.

Sam had described his house accurately, yet Joanna was still a little taken aback at how well maintained and lovely it looked: a gleaming white rambling farmhouse with a wide front porch and black shutters on the windows. She was also taken aback when Sam opened the door. Framed in the doorway, the light playing on his features, he looked especially handsome tonight. There was a soft scent of lemon in the air. Joanna wasn't sure whether it was his shampoo or aftershave, but she knew it was very nice. She also knew that it hadn't been pride or a pleasant chat with Penelope or that single place setting at her cabin that had kept her going on that long walk. It was Sam.

"I almost drove down the road to meet you," he said as he stepped aside to let her in.

"I wish you had," she admitted.

"Can I drive you home later?"

Joanna eyed him squarely as they stood together in the entryway. "You'd better. My feet are killing me."

They both laughed. Then Sam bent down and took a gentle hold of her left ankle, eased off her low-heeled shoe, and then removed the other shoe.

"Better?"

Joanna nodded, but she wasn't completely sure. Sam's gesture had been tame enough, but it had produced an uncomfortably intimate sensation as well as a fleeting thought about what it would be like if he continued undressing her. She couldn't ignore the truth of just how good it might feel.

"Where's Penelope?" Joanna asked. She might well need a chaperon tonight if the look in her eyes resembled the look in Sam's. He stood a couple of inches away from her, still dangling her shoes in his hand and smelling divinely of freshly squeezed lemons.

"She's finishing up some chores, and then she'll be along. How about a drink?" He led her into a large, attractive living room and placed her shoes neatly by the fireplace. There was a pleasant clutter of mix-and-match furniture, books, paintings, odd scatter rugs over a well-worn oak floor, giving the room a comfortable, lived-in feeling. Joanna walked over to the large brick hearth and warmed her hands near the crackling fire.

"I'll have a glass of wine," she said, looking up at the painting of a fair-haired, pretty young woman seated on a couch. Joanna recognized the couch as one of the two in this room.

"Red or white?"

"What, no rosé?" She turned to face him.

"I could probably dig up a rosé down in my wine cellar." He shook his head. "But you don't look like the rosé type to me."

"How come?"

"You're too decisive, too—"

"Black or white?" She smiled, turning back to the hearth. "Not in all things," she said more softly. Then she laughed. "White would be great."

Sam poured the straw-colored wine and walked over to Joanna with her glass.

"Your wife?" she asked, gesturing to the painting.

"Yes. That was done a few months after we were married."

Something about the tone in Sam's voice made Joanna realize he did not care to have any further discussion on the topic of his wife.

Joanna moved to the couch—not the one pictured in the painting. Her curiosity was stirred, but she did not ask any other questions. Sam sat down at the other end of the couch she had chosen.

65

"You have a beautiful home," she commented. Although she meant it, the words came out stiltedly, and she smiled uncomfortably.

"I have a feeling that when we first met, you pictured me living in something less . . . respectable," Sam said with a teasing smile.

Joanna laughed spontaneously, the awkwardness vanishing. "I thought you were some moderately illiterate and immodestly conceited farmhand who probably herded cows out to pasture for a living."

"You're fifty percent right. I do herd cows out to pasture."

"That was only my initial impression. I was pretty sure a few minutes after that first meeting that you were reasonably literate. You were too glib not to be."

"The Farmer's Almanac?"

"Right. Plus ads with sexy women in them."

"I've got eclectic reading habits. I also like science fiction, and when I'm in the mood, which I admit isn't too often, I read *The Wall Street Journal.*"

"You are a man of varied tastes," Joanna said.

"You mean a conceited man."

"I notice you haven't denied it."

"Denied what?" A voice piped up from across the room.

Both Sam and Joanna looked over their shoulders at Sam's daughter. Penelope's pigtails were undone, her soft brown hair falling loosely past her shoulders. The jeans and shirt had been replaced by a soft gray wool jumper and lace-trimmed white blouse. Joanna was struck not only by how much older and prettier Penelope looked tonight but by the striking resemblance she now observed between the girl and the painting of her mother.

"Well now, don't you look pretty." Sam beamed. "I think the last time I saw you all dressed up like this was when I dragged you to that school dance in the spring."

"Don't remind me of that disaster," she said with a smirk as she crossed the living room to join them. "That was the night Billy Jenks drank too much fruit punch and got sick all over the gym floor and all over—"

"We get the picture," Sam interrupted, laughing.

"I haven't been able to look at red punch since then without feeling a little queasy." Penelope giggled.

"Keep talking about it, and neither will we," her father answered. "At least I'm not serving punch tonight."

Penelope sat down across from Joanna, primly smoothing her skirt.

"You do look lovely. That's a great blouse. I have one something like it," Joanna said.

"Maybe you could show it to me sometime."

"Well, I left it home . . . I mean, in New York. I—I didn't think I'd be wearing it much up here."

There was an uncomfortable silence.

"I didn't realize you'd kept your place in the city," Sam commented in what he hoped was a casual way. Why was he so surprised she hadn't completely moved in up here? He never doubted she would eventually return to—to her home.

"I sublet my apartment for a year, furnished, and stored the clothing I wouldn't need here with friends."

"What happens when the year is over?" Penelope asked curiously.

"I'm not sure," Joanna admitted.

"You'll probably move back to New York. Right, Sam?"

Sam looked from his daughter to Joanna. *Right,* he thought. Out loud he said a little stiffly, "I'm not a mind reader."

"You were the one who said Jo would be bored silly in Brandon."

"We both know what I said. Now all three of us know." His scowl was softened by the teasing glint in his eyes. "Did you do all your school-work, Penelope?"

"Whenever he says 'Penelope' like that"—she sighed, casting her eyes upward in Jo's direction —"I start counting the days till my sixteenth birthday. He was the one who saddled me with the name in the first place. My mom wanted Lyla." She grimaced. "Personally I think they're both awful, but I had no say in the matter."

"If I remember correctly, you didn't talk too much at that point. Gosh, those were nice days," he said teasingly.

Penelope turned to Joanna. "What would you

68

do, Jo, if your folks had tagged you with a name like Penelope?"

"Actually your name is coming into vogue again. If you want to know the truth, I happen to like Penelope."

"I think the two of you are in cahoots." She eyed them suspiciously.

"Go see if Mildred has supper ready, will you . . . Penelope?" Sam ordered with a laugh.

As Penelope trotted off, Joanna peered at Sam. "And I thought you were a poor country boy."

"You mean Mildred? She cooks for me only when I have company. Beyond grilling a steak and throwing a vegetable or two into a pot, I'm not much of a chef."

"I like steak and vegetables. You didn't have to hire a cook to please me."

"I wasn't sure how to please you," he said more softly, "but I felt like trying my best." His eyes lit up mischievously. "Especially after I made you trudge over here."

"You didn't make me do that. I helped set myself up for that hike."

Penelope popped in to say that dinner would be ready in fifteen minutes and that she was going to help Mildred finish getting things ready.

"How often do you need Mildred?" Joanna asked after Penelope skipped off.

"Are you asking me how often I entertain beautiful young women . . . or how frequently

I have company over in general?" Sam asked jokingly.

"Beautiful young women, of course," she admitted with an impish grin.

"Mildred has never cooked for anyone quite like you before, Jo." He moved closer to her on the couch, the sudden desire to touch her so strong that he reached over and stroked her cheek with the palm of his hand.

Joanna was thrown by the unexpected intimacy. She looked at Sam for an answer to a question she hadn't quite formulated. His expression, however, held no answer.

She reached over to the coffee table for her wineglass and took a sip. The gesture was as much to moisten her dry throat as to lessen the sensual tension that was developing so rapidly between them. His touch had not left her cold by any means. But Joanna had no intention of responding to the message she was reading in Sam's warm gaze or to the one she was receiving clearly from her own body.

When Sam stood up and walked over to pour himself some more wine, she had the feeling he was no more inclined than she to let this attraction get the upper hand. But the realization did not produce the relief she expected. A hint of disappointment remained, even though she was glad Sam seemed as concerned as she was about stepping into hot water.

"We are going to talk plumbing sometime tonight, aren't we?" Joanna asked softly.

Sam was smiling down at her. "I think we'd better."

For the next ten minutes Sam answered Joanna's questions about installing her shower, even drawing her a few diagrams of the procedure. The conversation continued in the dining room after Penelope had called them both to dinner.

Mildred greeted Joanna cheerfully. While she served them all large helpings of chicken with light, fluffy dumplings, fresh string beans, and carrots, Joanna went over the whole plumbing procedure with Sam once more.

"It sounds as if you have it down cold."

"Now I just have to be able to apply what I know."

"Sam's great at plumbing," Penelope piped in. "He just installed a whole new watering system down at the east barn. You could put in a simple shower, couldn't you, Sam?"

"I could. I've already offered my services. Joanna is a very independent lady. She's a firm believer in doing things for herself." Sam's voice was slightly teasing, but Joanna thought she also heard a hint of respect in his tone.

"I came up here to see if I could survive on my own," Joanna started to explain to Penelope.

"Oh . . . an experiment? Are you doing this for a book or TV or—"

"I'm doing it for me. In a way it's an experiment. It's also a way to get in touch with nature . . . and with myself. I want to learn new skills, feel a sense of accomplishment in being able to

71

do things completely on my own. It's probably a little hard for people here to understand."

"No, it isn't," Penelope said. "Sam's been giving me that speech since I can remember. That's why I now have half a zillion chores to do around this place. I'm learning self-reliance, independence—"

Sam laughed. "And she's earning money for those ski boots."

"I'm not so sure it's worth it," Penelope grumbled. "Oops. I almost forgot. When I was helping Kenny this afternoon, he told me to let you know the new separator isn't working right. He wants you to check it out before the morning milking."

"Did he also say how those three new Holsteins are doing?"

"Better. He still thinks the littlest one is not gaining the way it should, but the other two are settling in nicely."

Penelope turned to Joanna. "You have to come over during the day sometime and see the place. We don't have a huge dairy like the ones out West, but for this area ours is one of the biggest. Definitely the best."

Joanna smiled and said she'd love to come over and see the operation of the farm. She was exaggerating, the notion of dairy farming not being high on her list of interests. In fact, as Penelope and Sam continued their discussion, catching up on the dairy news of the day, Joanna found herself distinctly bored and uncomfortably disconnected from the conversation.

The situation didn't improve much when Penelope switched from cow feed to curfews or when Sam chewed Penelope out for her hourlong telephone conversation with her girl friend the night before. While Penelope argued for having her own phone, Joanna found herself drifting off to memories of other dinner dates at friends' homes in New York. There the conversations had revolved around the latest movies or plays, politics, advertising, or the newest best sellers. Yes, she had sometimes been bored at those dinner parties, but at least there she could always relate to what people were discussing. Dairy farming and the plights of adolescence were subjects as far removed from her scope of knowledge as New York City felt right now from Brandon.

". . . *Stranger in a Strange Land,*" Sam said.

"What?" Joanna gasped. For a moment she thought Sam had ESP.

"I was suggesting Penelope use that book for her school report. It's a classic science fiction novel by Robert Heinlein."

"Yes. I—I've heard of it," Joanna stuttered.

"I'll bet you feel a bit like that yourself up here."

Joanna cocked her head to the side. Maybe he did have ESP after all. "When I do feel like a stranger, I remind myself of the pluses of living in a strange land."

"Like learning how to use a plane?" He grinned.

Joanna relaxed. "Only the kind that smooths wood. Although I might take up flying one day."

Sam laughed. "I believe, Miss Winfield, you could do anything you set your mind to."

"Tell me that after you see my new indoor shower and I might believe you."

The conversation moved to gossip Penelope had gleaned from the latest *People* magazine, the new thriller down at the local movie theater, and an article Sam had read in the paper about the upcoming local elections. Joanna found herself participating actively in the discussion, her earlier feeling of boredom and disassociation vanishing. By the end of the delicious dinner she discovered somewhat to her surprise that she was enjoying herself thoroughly.

Sam sent Penelope off to do her homework, but not before she countered with a couple of minutes of fruitless arguing. Before she begrudgingly left the room, Joanna reminded her to stop by to visit whenever she liked. Penelope gave Sam a "see, I told you so" look as she walked out.

"And I once thought raising a little kid was tough. It's nothing compared to coping with an adolescent." He sighed dramatically. "Whenever I feel like a stranger in a strange land with Penelope, I also try to remember the pluses."

Joanna studied him critically. "Oh, I'll bet you come up with a few."

"You're right. When we're not in the throes of an argument over curfews, telephones, and homework, we have a pretty terrific life together."

"You've been a twosome for a long time," Joanna commented, fishing for information.

"My wife died about thirteen years ago. It's been just me and Penelope since then," he said in a crisp, matter-of-fact way that again severed the conversation.

Sam smiled across at her as Joanna pushed aside her half-eaten slice of apple pie.

"I'm stuffed. Will Mildred's feelings be hurt if I don't finish this?" she asked.

"She'll never know. She left a few minutes ago."

Joanna stood up. "Then I'll help you do the dishes. I need to work off some of those calories."

Sam caught hold of her hand. "I'll do the dishes myself . . . later. I'm as self-sufficient and self-reliant as you are." He winked. "Besides, you don't need to work off any calories," he added with a wry smile.

"What do we do then? Stand here holding hands across the table?" She colored slightly but did not make any move to disengage Sam's tightened grip.

"No. Let's hold hands while we take a walk outside," he said softly. "I'll keep it under a mile."

"As long as you're still driving me home."

Sam let go of her hand. Joanna retrieved her shoes from the living room and let Sam help her pull on her jacket.

Once out the back door they walked along a path that ringed an open field. The autumn night air was chilly, and Joanna didn't argue when Sam put his arm protectively around her instead of holding her hand. She looked up at the star-filled sky and shivered slightly as his fingers skimmed her neck.

"Are you too cold?"

"No. It feels good." She paused, aware he could interpret that remark in more than one way. Then again, she'd meant it in more than one way.

He stopped walking and turned to face her. For a long moment he gazed at her without speaking.

"Starry eyes," he whispered.

"It's only a reflection," she whispered back.

He shook his head slowly, eyebrows raised, and spoke her name so softly she wasn't sure she'd heard it. Then all at once she was in his arms, his lips capturing hers in a tender yet demanding kiss. When he released her, Joanna's eyes were even brighter than before.

"Why did you do that?" she murmured. The tone in her voice bore no resemblance to the tone she'd used that first day when he'd kissed her at the cabin and she'd demanded to know why.

"Because it's damn near all I could think about this whole evening."

"Is it out of your system now?" she asked, feeling weak as he lifted his fingers through her hair.

"Not by a long shot."

She laughed, slipping her arms around his neck. "Maybe we'd better try again."

This time she parted her lips and shivered with pleasure as his tongue met hers. He pulled her tightly to him, locking her in a powerful embrace. Joanna let her body melt against Sam's as she gave herself up to the intoxicating feel of the kiss and to the warm sensation of being held so close. When they finally parted, he took hold of her hand and placed a chaste kiss on her palm.

"Kissing you could become a dangerous habit. What would I do when you returned to the big city?"

"I haven't made plans to return—at least not for a while," she whispered, chilled now that he had let her go.

"By that time the habit could be really tough to break. I was an impossible human being when I quit smoking. Ranted and raved for months. I couldn't put myself through something like that again."

"I'm trying to break a few habits of my own," Joanna admitted, "so I think I can understand what you're talking about. I vowed when I left the city that I was going to start depending on myself and not on some man for—for everything from plumbing to defining my identity as a worthwhile human being. And here I am, only a few weeks later, already swooning in the arms of the best-looking man in town. In another few minutes I'll probably be asking you to help me put that shower in or chop down that dumb fir

77

tree I've been working at for the past three days now or—or—"

"Or make passionate love to you when I take you back home?" he murmured with a boyish smile.

"That, too . . . maybe." She had to laugh. "I do find you terribly attractive, Sam Chase. But don't go getting any ideas that I'm—"

"Some wanton city woman." He finished the sentence for her, resting his hands on her shoulders. "I find you terribly attractive, too, Miss Joanna Winfield, and I assure you, I am no wanton country boy. I told you once before I take my romancing seriously."

"I came up here for the simple life, Sam. I *am* that stranger in a strange land you talked about before. But I'm slowly getting used to the place, and I like the way I'm beginning to feel about myself. I'm afraid romance would be too complicated for this new life-style of mine." She moved a few steps away from him. "I'm glad we've had this talk. We both know where we stand and—and I feel I can respect—"

The rest of her words were lost as Sam all at once grabbed her and roughly gathered her into his arms for another kiss—this one deeper and more passionate than the others.

Flushed and shaken by the force of Sam's action as well as by the response of her body to that force, she stammered, "Why—why did you —do that?"

Sam sighed. "One final try to get it out of my system. . . . It didn't work. Come on. I'd better take you home, neighbor, before I forget what a serious-minded guy I am."

He took Joanna's hand and led her around to the side of his house where his car was parked.

Walking to Sam's earlier, Joanna had fervently wished the distance were shorter. Now she wished the opposite as he pulled up at her door just a couple of minutes after they'd started the ride. She hadn't even had the chance to organize her thoughts before Sam was opening her door to let her out.

He gave her another chaste kiss, this one on the cheek, and started back around to his side of the car.

"Sam?"

"We're probably going to feel much better about my going home now when we wake up in our own bedrooms with our independence intact tomorrow morning, Jo. But right this minute, I feel like a teen-age boy who's been necking half the night with the girl of his dreams and has to hurry home to take a cold shower."

"Well, at least you can take a shower," she said with a laugh. "That's more than I can do tonight." She started toward her door and then paused. "You're probably right about tomorrow morning." She looked at him over her shoulder, a mischievous smile on her lips. "But what do we do if you're wrong?"

"If I'm wrong, you might have to reevaluate that survival plan of yours, and I might have to learn to get used to stepping into very hot water."

CHAPTER FIVE

A year before not only had Joanna known nothing about chopping down trees, but the thought of trying it had never entered her head. Today, large bow saw in hand, she heard the first cracking sound of a tree about to come crashing to the ground. She quickly moved out of the way. Standing back, she watched the trunk slowly tip and then topple. The fir tree she'd been working on for days had been felled, at last, by her own two hands.

There was something majestic and eloquent about the experience for Joanna. For a long while she sat on the stump of the fallen tree, relishing a sense of accomplishment unlike any she'd ever experienced before. With the sleeves of her flannel shirt rolled up, she could see the way the muscles in her arms had strengthened. In the past month she had grown thinner and unbelievably stronger. The physical work had done wonders for her body and her mind.

In this tiny little world she was creating, nurturing, where she was surviving pretty much on her own, she was also discovering a new freedom. She had never felt healthier or more vital.

Not that she wasn't ever lonely. She still knew very few people in the area. The more the local people saw her about, the friendlier they acted, but conversations were still brief and limited. She and Sam had also maintained their distance. He had not been around since their dinner together at his house the week before. No doubt he didn't care for cold showers in late October. She missed him. She had also grown more curious about him since that night. She wondered about his marriage, why he chose not to talk about his wife, whether he'd ever thought about marrying again.

Joanna told herself these were idle thoughts, a natural curiosity about a man she found appealing and attractive. But not someone, she insisted to herself, she wanted to become emotionally attached to.

She heard the sound of a truck pulling into her driveway. Having grabbed her plaid wool hunting jacket up from the ground, she slipped it on and broke into a run through the woods. She had been waiting impatiently for her plumbing supplies to arrive at Webster's hardware store so she could start her shower installation. Bob Webster had promised delivery as soon as he got her order in.

A battered red pickup truck was parked in front of the cabin. Joanna could see someone dropping the rear gate of the truck and pulling off a long plastic pipe. Webster had come through for her.

Only it wasn't Bob or one of the men from the hardware store unloading the truck.

"Hope you've got your illustrated guidebook memorized. You're set to roll." Sam set the pipe against the side of the truck and leaped easily onto the rear gate to lift up a rectangular molded section of fiberglass for the shower stall. "Give me a hand."

Joanna grabbed one end. "You didn't have to bring this stuff out. Bob Webster said he wouldn't mind delivering it." She backed up as she spoke, almost tripping on the pipe.

"Watch your step." He jumped from the truck, a broad grin on his face when he looked down at her feet. "I see you bought yourself some work shoes."

She laughed. "They didn't have any with steel tips in my size, but these are better than sneakers. I've also learned to watch out for falling doors."

"A woman who learns from experience," he said, nodding. "Where do you want all this stuff?"

"You can just get everything off the truck, and I'll find a place for it all."

"Joanna, are you sure you don't want a little extra manpower on this job? You are going to have to dig a trench outside to a drainage hole, break through some floor joists, and tear into studs in half your walls before you even set your first pipe in the ground."

"Come with me, Mr. Chase." She took his hand and guided him out to the back of the house. Pointing to a long, narrow trench in the ground, she said proudly, "A simple chore—only took me two days and a dozen sore muscles—but there it is." She whipped her tape measure off her belt in a motion akin to that of a sheriff grabbing for his six-shooter and with a twist of her wrist unreeled a stretch of tape, which she slipped into the trench.

Sam bent down to examine the measurement. "Four feet precisely. I'm impressed."

"No frozen pipelines for me this winter," she crowed. "I am safely below the frost line. And I'll bet you thought I'd never even heard of a frost line."

Sam started to speak, but Joanna pressed her fnger to his lips. "Wait, Mr. Chase. You haven't seen anything yet." She led him through the back door to the cabin. One corner of the room, the area that led to the small bathroom, looked as though a large family of chipmunks had gotten loose in the place and eaten half the walls and floors.

"It may not be the neatest job," Joanna admitted as Sam stood there speechless, "but once I finish, no one but you will ever know what it looked like at the start."

Sam walked over to get a closer look. Besides the gaping holes in the floor and walls, she'd left half a dozen beautifully executed drawings pinned to what walls still existed. He studied them carefully, discovering a skillful series of diagrams that laid out the entire plan in minute detail. When he turned around to Joanna, he saw a woman bursting with pride and enthusiasm and looking even more beautiful than she had when he'd first watched her hacking away at that closet door.

He wanted to walk over to her, take her in his arms, and tell her she was the best thing that had happened to him in many years. Except that he knew she could as easily shift to become the worst. He had spent the week counting all the ways the worst could happen. Number one on his list was the fact that home to Joanna was still New York. She had that lacy blouse in storage there, waiting for her return. For a while these past few days Sam had tried to talk himself into accepting a casual affair with Joanna, but in a town like this, what with his position as a businessman and father of a fifteen-year-old girl, it would not be a very wise choice. A more potent obstacle was that he already felt more than casual toward this beguiling city slicker.

Looking at her now, aglow with life, incredibly appealing in an oversize hunting jacket and mud-stained jeans, he found it hard to believe this wasn't the place Joanna belonged. He even began adjusting his earlier percentages. He wasn't sure how far in the other direction his adjustments went, but he was certain Joanna was no longer ninety-nine percent city.

"Country life agrees with you," he said with a smile.

"The other day, when I looked at myself in

the mirror," she said, walking toward him, "I almost didn't recognize me." She slipped off her jacket and extended an arm toward him. "I have muscles I never knew were lying dormant in this body of mine. Feel that bicep," she commanded, flexing her arm.

Sam slipped his large hand around the muscle. "You feel terrific." He didn't let go.

"I've missed you, Sam. Do you think we can . . . cope with this attraction business . . . and learn to be friends?"

"Do you have a simple illustrated guidebook for that project? If we're supposed to learn this one by doing, I'm afraid the action I have in mind isn't going to produce the results we say we want."

"Oh, Sam." She sighed. "I've accomplished so much up to now. I don't want to risk upsetting an applecart I've been carefully filling for the last month." She stepped back. Sam let go of her arm as she looked directly at him. "I think you've been carefully filling yours for thirteen years now if I get the message right."

Sam shook his head slowly. "You are really something, Jo. I should have known that we shared a burning curiosity along with the rest we have in common." He touched her lightly on the shoulder, his expression pensive.

"I didn't have a very successful marriage. I guess that's why I shy away from discussing it. It's not something I'm proud of. When Pam died in that car accident thirteen years ago, I wasn't in misery only over the loss. I had to accept a failure I'd kept hoping I could somehow turn into a success. I wanted to work things out with Pam. We both wanted that. But we never found a way." He gave Joanna a wry smile. "Maybe we needed one of your illustrated guides."

Joanna, touched by Sam's openness, gently took his hand. "I'm sorry, Sam."

"I'm not an easy man to live with. Ask Penelope. I was worse years back, when all I could think about was getting that farm of mine started. That goal took every ounce of energy I had. Took a lot away from my relationship with Pam. When we first started the farm, it was something we both wanted. But the more I lost myself in the work, the more Pam grew to resent it."

"Was she a city girl, too?" That would certainly explain a lot of Sam's caution where she was concerned.

Sam grinned. "Pam was born and bred in Brandon. Her father owned what is now Webster's hardware store. When Pam died, her folks sold the shop to Bob and retired down to Florida."

"So much for the obvious." Joanna smiled.

"In a way you've hit upon a sore spot that existed between me and Pam. Maybe because she'd always lived this kind of life, she never really valued it particularly. Not that she wanted to run off to Manhattan and become an ad exec." He gave her an amused smile. "No, Pam wanted a nice home, a family, peace of mind. She was pretty, sweet, and naïve. The truth is she married the wrong man. I was too driven back then, too caught up in my own need to fulfill my private dreams. I love my life, Jo. Between Penelope and my work most of my needs do get met."

"What about the rest?"

"They get met, too . . . just not on a permanent basis. In a small town like this either you marry the girl you start something up with or you go off to some other town to meet your needs. I didn't want another failed marriage, so I got familiar with some of the towns nearby."

Joanna sensed he was only half teasing her. "I guess we had better be really careful then since neither of us is in the market for getting married," she said, her eyes drifting up to Sam's.

"Of course, this time of day, most of the neighbors are off doing their chores." He took a step closer.

"No, Sam. We've gone over this ground before. I—I have my own chores to do. You must also."

"Right. Can't understand myself lately. You know, I looked into the mirror the other morning, and for a minute there I thought I was looking at some starry-eyed teen-ager. And I didn't have the reflection from the night sky to blame." He kissed her gently on the lips. "I'll stop by tomorrow to survey your new shower." Giving her a light, affectionate tap on her butt, he ordered, "Get to work."

When Joanna walked outside fifteen minutes later, she found all the pipes, fiberglass panels, and sundry clamps and valves neatly lined up against the side of the house. Now that she was actually ready to begin, the mass of supplies seemed intimidating. For quite a while she sat on the cold, hard ground, fumbling with the various parts, threading and unthreading pipes, testing the clamps, sorting out the T connectors from the ones with right angles.

Eventually she got the courage to begin. She started by cutting the pipes down to the right measurements with her hacksaw—a relatively easy task because she had opted to use plastic rather than copper or galvanized pipes. Putting the pipe clamps on was more difficult. She managed to tap the connector into the first pipe, but when she went to attach it to the second one, she had more difficulty. She was working up a good sweat, trying to twist the pipe into place, when Penelope stopped by on her way home from school.

"Need some help?"

A half hour ago Joanna would have turned her down, convinced she could handle this job easily on her own. Now she answered without hesitation, "Definitely." And then: "Don't tell Sam, though."

Penelope grinned. "I don't tell him everything. He is my father."

With the two of them pushing against each other and Joanna giving her pipe a twisting motion, success came quickly, the two pipes firmly in place under the connector. Joanna tightened a clamp over it and wiped her brow.

"Thanks a million, Penelope. I couldn't have done it without you. I think we both deserve a treat. Want a brownie?"

"Sure. But then I've got to hurry back. Chores," she explained and shrugged resignedly. "Another month, and I'll have the money for those boots. Then I'll have more time to visit."

Joanna was sorry to see Penelope go off so soon, but she was eager to get back to her work. Within the next couple of hours she managed to connect all the outside pipes and run them along the trench into the gravel-filled drainage hole fifteen feet from the house.

Before nightfall she was ready to move inside for the rest of the installation. Over dinner she studied her drawings, making sure she would be ready to tackle the work first thing the next morning.

As she sponged down that night, she smiled, realizing that at the same time tomorrow she could be standing in her brand-new indoor shower, luxuriating under the tingling spray. She also thought about Sam's stopping by to survey her handiwork. That led to other, more involved thoughts about Sam. Her mind replayed their conversation of this afternoon while her body replayed some of the responses he seemed to be stirring in her on a disturbingly regular basis.

After such a physically exhausting day Joanna should have slept a lot better than she did. As it was, she tossed and turned most of the night, fighting off dreams about Sam Chase.

The next morning, rested or not, she began work shortly after dawn. That nice, hot steamy shower was going to be hers tonight . . . or else. Several times that morning Joanna wished Penelope would magically appear like one of the cobbler's elves. Still, with her own two sore and calloused hands, Joanna continued at her labors, stopping only to have some lunch, keep logs going in the wood stove, and apply bandages to cut fingers. Her hands looked a little like an ad for Band-Aid adhesive strips by the time three o'clock rolled around. She was also dotted with dirt splotches, damp from perspiration and water, and utterly exhausted.

But she had the finest-looking indoor shower she had ever seen. And it worked. It actually worked. Following the last step in her handy illustrated guide, she went back through the house and outside, carefully checking for drips. Drips, the book reminded her in bold red lettering, could be disastrous to foundations and could waste water and rot out wood.

What the book didn't mention was that sometimes overzealousness could be far more disastrous than drips to home, hearth, and a person's sanity.

Joanna first spotted the drip just where she had placed one of her last clamps on the pipes between the sink and shower. She figured she had probably been running out of strength when she tightened it and simply hadn't turned it far enough. Fortunately it was an easy connection to get to, being in between two studs in the bathroom wall, which she had postponed enclosing until tomorrow.

She almost decided to let the drip wait as well, but then she remembered how her guide had warned her not to put off till tomorrow what could turn into a problem today.

Just as she decided to take care of the drip she saw Sam's truck pulling into the drive. She hurried to tighten the clamp, eager to show off her accomplishment.

Catastrophe timed itself perfectly to Sam's knock on the front door. The tiny drip suddenly erupted into a veritable geyser as Joanna gave the troublesome fitting one final turn. She screamed in surprise and panic, water gushing all around her. Her hands clung to the detached pipe, unable to contain even a fraction of the flow.

When Sam rushed through the house to the bathroom, he found Joanna standing in a good six inches of water, a fountain of spray shooting up to the ceiling and showering back down on her.

Luckily Sam spotted the shutoff valve almost immediately and turned the water off. Joanna was still holding the two ends of pipe, now no longer gushing water. A few final spurts trickled out and fell into the flood that was now streaming into the living room. Sam rushed around, lifting up rugs and hoisting the two upholstered chairs up on top of the kitchen table.

Joanna stood frozen, her mind still unable to take in the calamity that had so quickly replaced one of the great achievements of her lifetime. All that work . . . and she had forgotten to shut off the water.

Sam walked into the bathroom and gazed at the dripping wet shower stall and then at Joanna. He took the pipes from her hands and retrieved the fallen clamp.

"You should have used more pipe dope," he said softly.

His words brought her abruptly out of shock. She glared at him in outrage, frustration, and despair.

"Don't you dare call me a dope, you—you . . ." Tears streamed down her face, the reality of the disaster finally taking hold. All that work, time, cuts, and bruises . . . and now adding insult to injury, this man had the nerve to stand there and call her a dope.

He took her in his arms, holding her tight while she cried, too wiped-out to struggle against his embrace.

"Joanna," he whispered, wiping the grime off her cheek when the tears stopped, "I didn't call you a dope." He reached for the tube of compound lying on the edge of the sink. "This gray, gooey stuff you've been using to seal the threads on the pipes so they don't leak is affectionately known in the plumbing trade as pipe dope. You just didn't put enough on."

Joanna sniffed and looked down at the tube in

Sam's hand, then at their soaked shoes. Finally she met his tender gaze.

"I was doing so well. It looked . . . great," she muttered.

"We'll fix it, Jo. Water dries. Nothing's broken. You did a terrific job."

His soothing words only made her start to cry again.

"Tonight I was going to take my first real shower in a month. I have never in my life looked forward to a shower as I did to this one." She looked back up at him and saw the smile on his face.

"Go on, laugh. Little you know, living in that luxurious house with probably half a dozen showers and bathtubs and all the conveniences of—of home. . . ."

"You deserve a little of that luxury after all your hard work. There aren't six showers, but there are a couple back at the house you can choose from. You're also going to need a dry place to spend the night. And since you already told me I don't need Mildred to please your palate, we can throw some steaks on the grill for dinner."

Joanna eyed him with mild suspicion, but she didn't argue. The offer sounded too good, and she felt too miserable to turn down the meal, bed, and hot shower, no matter where that shower was located.

"Go change into some dry clothes, grab your toothbrush and whatever it is you sleep in, and I'll mop up."

"No, it's my disaster. I'll mop, and then I'll go change."

"How about a little neighborly help?"

Joanna smiled for the first time since disaster had struck. "Thanks."

They worked together for about twenty minutes. The damage hadn't been too bad. Sam made sure the water main was shut tight. Then he added the pipe dope to the threads and refastened the clamp.

"By tomorrow night you'll have your very own custom-built shower ready and waiting," he said as she sat down on her bed to remove her sodden work shoes. She struggled for a minute, and then Sam came over, knelt beside her, and removed both shoes.

"You seem to be getting lots of calls for taking off my . . . shoes," she said in an unsteady voice as he peeled off her wet tennis socks. Her cold feet were warming rapidly in his grasp.

Sam glanced up at her, then let his gaze travel down the front of her wet shirt and jeans. Joanna had no difficulty interpreting the message in that gaze. He was willing to continue being helpful. More than helpful.

Joanna was trembling. She felt cold and incredibly aroused at the same time. She wanted to get her wet clothes off, and she knew damn well she wanted Sam's help. She wanted Sam. Disaster not only had blown her perfect shower but had shot her defenses. Suddenly she could hear the sound of her own heartbeat.

She placed her hands on his face and leaned

toward him. Against his ear she whispered, "Sometimes a woman needs more than she wants to admit."

Sam kissed her neck, his hands moving up to her shirt. With deft fingers he undid the buttons and tugged it off. He continued removing all her wet things, swiftly threw back the covers on the bed, and tucked her beneath their warmth. It took him only seconds to remove his own clothes and slip in next to her, gathering her in his arms.

The warmth from his strong, muscular body outdid any amount of blankets. Joanna clung to him as he draped one leg over hers, cradling her against him. He ran his hands up and down her body first in a vigorous motion to stop the chill and then slowly, languorously as he felt her stop shivering and begin responding to his touch.

Sam's embraces, his kisses, his every touch felt so right, so natural that Joanna found herself responding without hesitation or doubt. She had already admitted loving the way he looked. Now she discovered she loved the way he felt even more. His body was taut, lean, muscular— not from hours of lifting barbells in some gym but from the sweat of hard honest labor. His strength and power had an intoxicating effect on her senses. Even the subtle aroma of hay, replacing the heady lemon scent from the other night, excited her. She thought him the most masculine man she had ever met. The warmth of his body merged with hers as they held onto each other, each knowing that this moment had been inevitable, the culmination of weeks of fantasy and dreams.

Her hands felt his muscles ripple beneath her touch. She pressed her lips against his throat, her fingers trembling down his chest to his hard, firm stomach. She moved lower, her face pressed to his heart, her hands on his thighs as he gently tugged her dampened hair away from her neck and bent low to kiss her moist flesh.

He laid her back on the bed, letting his eyes rest for a moment on her finely etched features, and then he brushed her eyelids, cheeks, and mouth with light, tender kisses. Her lips curved into a sensual smile as he ran his tongue from one corner of her mouth to the other.

Joanna arched her back as his lips moved down the slender curve of her throat to her rounded breasts, her nipples hard against his cheek and then against his tongue as he took first one, then the other into his mouth, savoring the taste and the feel of her.

She thrust her slender fingers through his hair, holding him captive against her bosom, wanting the sensations he was stirring inside her to go on forever. He slipped his large hand between her thighs, and her legs parted at his gentle prodding. Joanna cried out with sharp pleasure as he continued his sensual caresses.

Poised on a precipice, she sensed his lovemaking carrying her ever closer to the edge. Her passion and need fired her own explorations. All her discoveries sweetened the ecstasy. Not only was he an expert giver of pleasure, but he responded with complete openness and joy as she made love to him. Joanna had never experienced such an honest, loving interaction with any other man.

When they came together, it was in the same natural way they had first embraced. In rhythm, pace, and eagerness they were perfectly matched. Joanna opened her eyes for a brief moment to see Sam's gaze on her, his eyes filled with open passion and utter tenderness. She cried out in pleasure, her body shuddering beneath his as they traveled together over the brink of the precipice.

Joanna smiled as she curled against him. Wasn't she the one who'd said she was here to learn by doing? Nothing less would have helped her understand the exquisite sensations Sam had taught her today. He had turned sheer disaster into total bliss.

Sam laughed contentedly as Joanna lifted herself onto her elbow and gazed down at him. She grinned. "I never realized what a terrific neighbor you were going to be."

"I told you on that first day that to know me was to love me," he said teasingly, pulling her to him for another kiss.

"I'm a little scared you might be right," she said, struggling free from his embrace. "This could get serious. What are we going to do?"

"If the townsfolk get wind of this affair, I'm going to have to make an honest woman out of you or they just might run you out of town."

"I may run out of town on my own steam if things get too complicated. I told you—"

"I know, Jo. You want the simple life."

"I don't know exactly what I want at this point. Ten minutes before you arrived today I was surveying my brilliant piece of plumbing and I felt I was really beginning to belong here. Then, minutes later, standing in water up to my ankles, I wondered what had ever possessed me to leave my nice, dry apartment in Manhattan."

"And now?"

"Now . . . I feel completely at home in your arms. But then this could be merely a momentary illusion. Another catastrophe could befall me at any turn. I have seemed to be disaster-prone since I moved up here. Nothing like this ever happened to me in New York."

"Nothing like this has ever happened to me in Brandon," Sam whispered seductively, intentionally misinterpreting her words.

Joanna grinned, putting her arms around Sam's neck. "Who would have guessed just how many unique experiences were awaiting me when I decided to embark on my pioneering adventure?"

"You have to admit, discovering new talents has its rewards."

She couldn't argue that. In fact, she was more than ready to test those talents once again.

CHAPTER SIX

"Penelope seemed awfully subdued tonight," Joanna said thoughtfully as she helped Sam gather the dishes off the table.

"I have a feeling she's getting a bit suspicious. Two months is a long time to keep . . . things under wraps." He gave her a warm smile, but Joanna picked up the note of concern in his voice.

"Maybe you should talk to her. Lately she hasn't been over to my place very often. She could be nervous about finding you there, although I think we've been pretty careful, don't you?" Joanna set a stack of dishes back down on the table and turned to face Sam.

Ever since that fateful afternoon when her shower exploded, Joanna had given up her fight to maintain a purely neighborly relationship with Sam. They'd spent endless hours talking about the repercussions of getting involved, agreeing to keep their new intimacy quiet at least until they knew where it was going to lead.

Sam came closer and kissed her gently on the lips. "Have you taken a good look at yourself

99

recently? Or me? We've both got so many stars in our eyes we beat out Old Glory. Do you really think there's one person in this town, including Penelope, who doesn't know we're . . . crazy about each other?"

Joanna grinned. "I guess it's all pretty obvious, even if you do park down the road and sneak in my back door during chore time."

"You're my favorite chore of the day," he said seductively, grabbing her for a deeper, hungrier kiss.

Joanna struggled out of his embrace. "What if your daughter walked in now?"

"She's down at the north barn, checking on that pregnant cow." He pulled her back to him.

This time she circled her arms around his neck, returning his kiss with equal passion.

They held each other close. "What do you think about chickens?" Joanna asked suddenly.

Sam laughed. "Chickens? Is that what kissing me makes you think about?"

"Uh-huh," she said jokingly. "It's a natural progression." She held up a tiny reed of hay plucked from his shoulder. "So what do you think, Farmer Brown? You're the animal expert."

"Cows, not chickens."

"Did I ever tell you the story about my uncle the chicken farmer?" She jabbed him in the ribs playfully.

"How did he make out?"

"The family disowned him one Christmas when we got a large carton filled with frozen chicken legs. I think he sold the business the next year and went into oil wells." She cocked her head, her expression pensive. "Now that's another possibility."

"Vermont has never been noted for its oil wells. But something tells me you'd have more luck digging holes than raising baby chicks." A disturbing thought drifted into his mind.

"What is it, Sam?"

He tried to keep his voice light when he answered. "Raising chickens isn't a casual affair, Jo. It—it takes commitment. Anything you do up here does."

Joanna met Sam's gaze. This was not the first time in the past two months that the subject of commitment had come up. Sam had made it clear from the start that he was a serious-minded guy. It wasn't that she took her relationship with him lightly, but for now she was happy with the way things were going. Letting a day at a time unfold felt good to her. In New York her life-style constantly demanded planning ahead, working toward a future goal, a future deadline, and a future marriage on a couple of occasions.

Up here Joanna felt she was beginning life all over again. With new discoveries, new skills, her sense of well-being grew daily. Instead of deadlines, schedules, planned dates, organized activities, she took each day as it came. Life now meant chopping wood for her fire, starting seeds indoors for her garden, repairing leaks now that she had finally passed her plumbing apprenticeship. She was becoming quite a nifty carpenter, too. Last week she had made herself a new coffee table to replace the sadly lopsided one old Mr. Harvey had left in the cabin. Tomorrow she was going to begin insulating her small attic space in an effort to conserve heat.

Every day produced simple joys, revelations, an appreciation of the smallest happenstance, an awareness of the wonder and power of nature. Her sense of self-sufficiency was even allowing her to lean toward getting a telephone installed in the cabin. So far she had carefully guarded against too much input from her friends in the city. She wrote brief letters, more often postcards, and received chatty mail in return. Her friends, most of them still unable to believe she could survive out in the sticks, were curious about how she was doing.

Joanna was doing more than surviving. But because this experience was still an adventure to her, she could not yet give the commitment she knew Sam wanted. Despite her happiness, she recognized that she was not ready to set down roots. There was a part of her she couldn't deny that still missed some of the excitement, the new happenings, the glamour of Manhattan. Sometimes she felt an urge to stop in at an art gallery or play hooky for the day and take in a matinee. When she visited the local library in Brandon and was told the book she'd ordered wasn't in yet, she remembered with longing the New York Public Library.

Sam had continued clearing the table. When

he walked back in from the kitchen, Joanna carefully lifted up the linen place mats.

"I'd better think some more about those chickens before I get into something over my head." She saw the flash of disappointment in Sam's face, but he didn't press the issue.

"Do you want me to pick up that insulation roll for you at Webster's tomorrow morning?" he asked lightly, taking the mats from her.

"Yes. That would be great. I've been thinking of your offer to sell me that old truck. It would save my having to depend on you and Bob to transport things out to the cabin for me."

"You sure that isn't making too big a commitment?" The sarcasm rang through despite his vow to keep his feelings under control.

"I could always sell it. Trucks move better than chickens." She took a deep breath. "Let's not fight, Sam."

"We're not fighting, though maybe a good knock-down, no-holds-barred fight is what we need," he said, but his eyes held only warmth and tenderness.

When he looked at her like that, Joanna felt weak in the knees. "I am crazy about you, Sam."

He nodded. It would work out, or it wouldn't. Ultimately a decision was going to have to be made. Sam understood that this was not the time to push, as much as he wanted to grab hold of her and force her to see that she belonged here with him. In his heart he had grown to believe Joanna was setting down some strong roots without even realizing it. Brandon was be-

103

coming a part of her soul as it was a vital part of his. But if he forced the issue before she shared his awareness, he knew she could bolt and flee.

"Sam! Sam!" Penelope's panicked call resounded along with the banging of the back door. "I think something's wrong with that cow. Kenny says to come quick. He rang up Doc Wilson, but *he's* out on a call in Dover. He probably won't get back tonight at all."

"Okay. Take it easy. Run out to the shed, and get me my emergency medical kit. Then grab some towels, and get Kenny and Tom to bring down a few buckets of warm, soapy water." He turned to Joanna. "You ever see a calf come into this world?"

She gave him a wry smile.

"Well, come on then. Let's hope we have one entering it tonight."

The blistery December wind mingled with a steady snowfall as Joanna and Sam made their way in the bitter cold down to the north barn.

The pregnant heifer was off by herself in a corner of the stall. Sam rushed directly over to her while Joanna hung back, her teeth chattering, her breath frosty even inside the relative warmth of the barn.

The others arrived, and everyone set to work —everyone but Joanna who was feeling completely out of her element and content to watch from a distance.

The poor cow was in obvious distress. Sam called out to Kenny that the calf was breech first, and he would have to try to manipulate it gently into a frontal position. Joanna could tell from Sam's tone that it would not be an easy thing to accomplish.

Penelope stood close to Sam, tenderly patting the pained cow on the flanks as her father carefully probed. She whispered soft, soothing words to the animal as her eyes filled with tears.

"Can you do it, Sam? Are they going to make it?"

"I hope so, Penelope. I think . . . easy, little mother . . . just a few more minutes . . . we don't want to hurt you now . . . okay . . . we're getting there." He smiled up at his daughter to reassure her.

If anyone could pull them through, Sam could. He'd done it before. Penelope reached for a small towel and wiped Sam's brow.

Finally he sat back, patting the cow gently. "Anytime now, folks." He looked over his shoulder at Joanna.

By her expression, Sam sensed that she found the experience somewhat overwhelming, and he did not urge her to join him for the birth.

It came quicker than he had guessed now that he had maneuvered the fetus into the correct position. The delivery itself was easy, but the newborn calf had suffered from its distorted placement in the uterus. It lay on the towels, a limp, helpless, matted creature, struggling for breath. Because the mother cow was so drained, and the calf sickly, Sam could not rely on the normal mothering instinct of the cow to tend to her newborn. He had to take a coarse towel and gently but vigorously rub the calf down to warm it and stimulate the blood flow. His efforts also served as a way of telling the baby it was loved.

Penelope took turns with Sam. She crooned softly to the calf, humming little tunes, whispering gentle loving words while she rubbed it with the towel.

Sam walked over to Joanna once he saw that the calf was beginning to come around.

He looked exhausted but exuberant. Joanna stifled the impulse to give him a congratulatory hug. "You're quite the obstetrician, Dr. Chase. I'm truly impressed."

"And truly wiped-out, I bet. It's after midnight. I've got to stay with Mom and the babe for the night." He reached into his pocket for the keys to the truck. "Here. Want to give the pickup a test drive?"

"I could stay with you if you like." Her offer had less than a ring of sincerity about it. She was half in awe of the event she had just witnessed but still overwhelmed as well. And for the first time in months she felt like a complete outsider in a world that was newly foreign again.

Sam watched Joanna leave the barn, a look of disappointment etched in his features. He had wanted her to share in the experience, to feel some of the excitement and wonder of it all. Over the years he had delivered several calves, and each time he himself felt a bit reborn. He turned back to his daughter, snuggled up with the new calf in her lap. She was half-asleep, content and secure in the world Sam had made for her. He sat down beside her, gently cradled her in his arms, and stared down at the new life he had helped bring into the world.

Joanna drove the two miles back to her cabin. As tired as she had been back at the barn, now she was edgy and tense. For the first time she had gotten a real taste of Sam's world—a world she knew he wanted her to share. And all she felt was disconnected and confused. *A stranger in a strange land,* she thought despairingly. For a while there that feeling had almost vanished. Almost, but not quite.

Standing in that barn tonight, Joanna understood more fully just what a commitment to Sam would mean. It required not only her promise to love enduringly a man she had so easily grown to love already but also her promise to become a new member of a ready-made, strongly established family, a promise to sit up nights with pregnant cows and sick calves, a promise to become a part of a world she barely comprehended.

That night she thought about New York with a homesickness she had not felt in a long, long time.

"I'm sorry, Jo. You should have told me earlier," Sam said, finishing his coffee.

"I wanted it to be a surprise."

"Can't you exchange the tickets for another night?"

Joanna sighed. "The show's in Burlington only for the night. I thought you'd enjoy seeing a play for a change. I haven't seen live people on a stage for four months now."

"Maybe someone else will go with you. Or you could go down there yourself, make a night of it, even stay over at the Holiday Inn or something and indulge in big-city luxury."

She gave him a snide smile. Burlington wasn't classified as a "big city" in her book.

"Look, Jo. I really am sorry. It's just that I promised Penelope we would take Saturday off to go up to Dover to get those ski boots. She's been working so damn hard for months, and the ski season is already well under way. You understand."

"Sure." She gathered the mugs. "No big deal. Maybe I will go alone."

He grabbed her arm and pulled her onto his lap. "I promise. Next time a live person appears on a stage within a hundred-mile radius of Brandon, I'll drop whatever I'm doing and take you there."

She kissed him gently on the lips, and her face softened into a smile. "I'll hold you to that promise."

He smoothed her hair and tucked a strand behind her ear. "Jo, if you miss the theater and all that so much, why not go into New York for a few days—fill up on culture and then . . . come home?"

"I've thought about that," she admitted, "more than once. Last week Gary Simms called. After bemoaning a long list of hassles at work, he told me about a new Neil Simon play he and his wife adored and an art show that featured the work of a mutual friend of ours. I felt jealous. I stood in front of the mirror afterward, and you know what I thought? I thought about the fact that I haven't gotten dressed up or had my hair done in more than four months. I look like a—"

"Like a country hick. A beautiful, strong, healthy, rugged mountain lass," he whispered seductively.

Joanna laughed softly, leaning her head on his shoulder. "Like a country hick, all right . . . with bunions, calluses, muscles that rival Mr. Universe's, scars from umpteen disasters—and . . . Sam! What are you doing?" she screamed when he suddenly began undressing her.

"I'm counting scars."

"Stop it," she pleaded, squirming in his arms as he started tickling her. "Your daughter is going to have her worst suspicions confirmed in another minute. She's coming over to help me bake bread."

Sam glanced down at his watch as he held her fast, then released her with a sigh. "You win this round. School got out fifteen minutes ago."

Joanna straightened her hair and quickly rebuttoned her flannel shirt. "Are you staying for a while?"

"That doesn't sound like an invitation."

"It isn't," she said. "Penelope and I are beginning to feel comfortable with each other again. I think she's getting used to the idea . . . of you and me being close. It's going to take time, though."

Sam put his arms around her. "I have all the time in the world," he murmured in her ear. "And don't forget, we've got a date for the very next play that comes along." He started toward the front door and paused. "If you'd rather pass up this play, you could come with us to Dover instead."

"No. It's a special father-daughter occasion. Besides, I've gone to a few plays alone in my time. And if I decide not to go, that'll be all right, too. I've survived this many months without culture. A few more can't hurt."

. . . *Much*, she thought as he closed the door.

Joanna did go to Burlington on Saturday night to see the show. It wasn't Broadway, but it wasn't bad. She knew she would have enjoyed it a lot more if Sam had come along, but she tried not to dwell on that point. She saw Bob Webster and his wife at the play. *At least some people in the town appreciate culture,* she thought wistfully.

That afternoon she had called Greyhound to find out its schedule to New York. She hung up before anyone came on the line. Then on the bus down to Burlington she argued with herself; it was ridiculous to be afraid to go to New York for a brief visit. But Joanna knew she was scared she might not make the round trip back to Brandon. She was in love with Sam, yet she felt completely torn between two worlds, as if she didn't really belong in either place. This little experiment in survival had turned her into the proverbial "man without a country."

Although it was after eleven when she returned from Burlington, Joanna decided to wash her hair. Her shower had spouted another leak, and she was still waiting for the part needed to repair it, so she was back to sponge baths again and none too happy about it. Washing her hair in the kitchen sink was a pain in the neck . . . literally and figuratively.

Sam walked in the front door just as she had finished towel-drying her hair and was trying to untangle the mass of snarls the vigorous rubdown had created.

"You've got great timing, Sam Chase," she snapped, throwing the towel back over her head and wrapping it turban-fashion.

He stood inside the door, laden with packages. One, a large bouquet of tea roses, was unwrapped.

"Christmas is over," Joanna said, softening. "And I wasn't angry enough at having to see that play alone tonight to warrant any bribes."

"Even a country hick needs a few luxuries," he replied with an endearing smile, extending the bouquet of roses.

Joanna took them from his hand. "They're beautiful, Sam. They couldn't have been easy to come by."

"They weren't." He was still smiling.

"What else did you bring?" She laughed as he held her away from the other boxes.

111

"Go put your flowers in water. Then fix your hair and light a couple of candles."

"Aye, aye, Farmer Brown."

Sam set down the two boxes, one large and one small and rectangular. He slipped a magnum of champagne out of the paper bag he was carrying.

"Sam, what's going on?" Joanna asked suspiciously as he carried a couple of wineglasses over to the coffee table.

"I'm only trying to do my best to share at least part of this night with you," he said softly.

"I'd better put on something other than this old robe if we're going to drink champagne by candlelight."

Sam took her hand and led her over to the large box he'd set down on the kitchen table. "Open it."

Joanna glanced up at him and then carefully undid the silver ribbon and shiny white wrapping paper. When she lifted the lid of the box and folded back the tissue paper, she saw an exquisite mauve silk chemise dress with delicately thin shoulder straps. It was at once simple and elegantly chic.

"I'm—I'm flabbergasted," Joanna sputtered.

"Your pal Penelope helped me pick it out. She said it was definitely you, and I had to agree."

"You're both right." Joanna lifted the dress out of the box and held it up against her.

"Put it on," he said, a tender smile on his lips, a hungry expression in his eyes.

Joanna's eyes sparkled. "How about a little help, neighbor."

Sam walked over to her to sweep her copper hair off her neck so that he could kiss his favored spot below each earlobe. He took the dress and laid it on the back of the chair, then pulled her to him, slipping his hands beneath the robe.

"No flannel gown tonight?" he whispered.

"I didn't feel like washing clothes today. Now I won't need that gown anyway—at least for the evening."

"Make that the entire night—if you want to see this mug of mine first thing in the morning, that is."

"Sam, do you mean it?" In all these months they had never spent an entire night together because of Sam's daughter.

"Penelope stayed in Dover for the night at a friend's house. I don't have to pick her up until tomorrow afternoon."

"Oh, Sam, I'm dying to see that mug of yours tomorrow morning," she whispered, breathless as his hands cupped her buttocks under her robe.

"I was hoping you'd say that," he said, then kissed the curled edges of her lips.

"Sam, let's not bother with the dress for now," she suggested softly.

"Oh, no. I didn't spend an hour feeling completely awkward in that little boutique to skip the pleasure of seeing you all dolled up . . . for a little while anyway." He eased the robe off her shoulders, and although his intentions were to help her dress, he allowed himself to get side-tracked for a few minutes.

When he finally slipped the dress over her head, Joanna growled, "You're a tease, Sam Chase. I don't feel like playing . . . dress-up right now."

The dress fitted her to perfection. The soft silk against her naked body felt deliciously wicked and looked much as it felt. She turned around slowly to give Sam a view from every angle. Her eyes traveled down his body and she grinned playfully when she noticed the obvious effect her appearance had on him.

She moved closer to him, but he backed up with a broad smile. "Slow down. I want to drink in your sophisticated splendor for a few minutes. Or else that dress won't stay on you long enough for me to remember what you look like in it."

"How can I look sophisticated without any shoes on?" She turned her head, remembering the other box on the kitchen table. "That's what's in the other package," she exclaimed, beaming. "You thought of everything." She reached for the box before Sam could stop her.

"It's not what you think, Jo." He chuckled at the expression on her face as she opened the lid and looked inside.

"Sam, you nut. You crazy, lovable nut." She turned to him with tears in her eyes. "Oh, Sam, they're beautiful."

"They don't go too well with that dress, but now I can stop worrying about some closet door falling on your foot again and breaking one of those toes I love so much."

Joanna looked up from the brand-new steel-tipped work shoes. "I adore you, Sam. This is the best damn present anyone has ever given me."

"I just hope you keep them on long enough to wear them out so I can buy you a second pair," he said, taking her in his arms.

"Sam, I—"

"Don't say anything now, Jo. I know I've put you at an unfair disadvantage. We'll talk in the morning . . . when we wake up together."

She wore the dress while drinking exactly one glass of champagne. By the time Sam poured the second glassful they were snuggled close together in Joanna's big bed.

"This was a perfect evening," she said, nestling in against his chest.

"It isn't over." He hugged her to him. "For once I don't have to rush home in the dead of night. I intend to watch the sunrise with you."

Joanna yawned, then giggled. "Well, you'll have to keep me busy until it comes up."

"Exactly what I had in mind."

He gently nudged her onto her back and began running his fingers lightly over her body. "You looked great in that dress, but you look even better without it."

"Isn't that one of the advantages of country life? You don't ever have to dress . . . up."

She pulled him down on top of her, kissing him urgently. "I never knew I was so greedy. I can't seem to get enough of you."

He stroked her breasts, then pressed his lips to a taut nipple, slipping one hand between her thighs. When he looked up into her eyes, he saw that she was watching him with exquisite pleasure.

"Isn't it nice that we have greed in common, too? I'd say we were meant for each other, Jo."

He intentionally gave her no opportunity to respond. Instead, she gasped as he slid inside her, the force of his powerful, rhythmic movements leaving her breathlessly aroused. She clung to him tightly, her body responding eagerly to his thrusts.

A soft cry escaped her throat as a wave of delicious spasms swept over her. Sam kissed her hard on the mouth, then dug his face into her neck. He cried out as he soared with her to the height of ecstasy. Joanna held him fast, her legs entwined around his thighs. Sam glided his hands down to her hips.

"You get stronger and more beautiful every day, Jo. I love the feel of your body. . . ."

"So much is different about me now, sometimes it's hard for me to remember that half-crazed ad exec who was always racing in and out of rush-hour subways, flying down corridors on the way to meetings, staring out an apartment window at a ridiculous blue air shaft."

"She was also the woman who went to the theater, galleries, museums, Bloomingdale's."

"I know," she said softly. "There's that, too." She gave him a wistful look. "Maybe you could start a dairy farm in Manhattan. Then we could spend half our time there and half here—the best of both possible worlds."

"I've got the best already, Jo. And I believe more and more, as I watch you thrive here, that you do, too. At some point you're going to have to make a choice."

"I don't feel ready to do that. Today I almost booked a Greyhound bus into the city. I'm scared, Sam. I don't know if I could ever be truly satisfied staying here permanently. Sure, four months ago I thought if I never saw another ad campaign in my life, I wouldn't care. But now, there are times I miss the job as well as the—the action." Her expression became wistful. "I don't want to rush back there tomorrow, take it all up again, but I do wonder if after a year . . ."

"Jo, the grass is always greener . . ."

"I know the saying. I just don't want to make any promises I might not be able to keep."

Sam kissed her and, with a weary smile, whispered, "The only promise I want you to make right now is that you'll wake up in my arms tomorrow morning."

"I promise."

Joanna kept her promise. When she woke up the next morning, the sun was just beginning to edge over the mountains and she was snuggled in Sam's arms. Looking up at him, she saw that he was already awake.

"How long have you been up?" she asked, her voice husky with sleep.

"Long enough to fantasize what it would be like to do this each day."

She nestled closer to him. "It does feel nice." For a few moments she let the same fantasy of their waking up together every morning drift through her mind. Then reality intruded.

"Any other morning you probably would have been down at the barn by this time. And I'd be racing around getting Penelope's lunch together, and then I'd probably be carrying my buckets over to the cows for milking."

Sam chuckled. "Those cows would be mighty lucky to get a milkmaiden like you. After years of mechanical operations they'd be in for quite a treat."

Joanna tossed a pillow on top of his head. Then she pulled it away and stared down at him, her expression serious. "Let's keep the fantasy on hold for a while."

Sam nodded, watching her scurry out of bed to stoke the logs in the wood stove. When she climbed back next to him, she was shivering. He held her close, savoring reality, forcing his fantasies aside.

CHAPTER SEVEN

On the spring morning Gary Simms showed up from New York for a surprise visit, Joanna's truck had broken down, her goat had escaped her painstakingly erected wire fence, and the previous night's storm had knocked out her electricity.

When she heard the car pull up, Joanna was in the middle of restaking the metal poles the goat had trampled. She was dressed in what had become her daily uniform: sturdy jeans (last year's designer jeans having long ago worn out), blue cotton work shirt, and her trusty steel-tipped work shoes, which she knew Sam was pleased to see were almost shot.

Gary Simms, dressed in crisp khaki chinos, creamy beige button-down shirt with a lamb's wool brown crew neck sweater draped around his neck and a pair of designer sunglasses casually propped on top of his head, looked so country casual Joanna had to laugh. Then she saw Gary's surprised expression, and the laughter stopped.

"Don't tell me. I look like a walking disaster.

You could have given me some warning, Gary." She paused, a broad smile breaking out. "But jeez, I'm glad to see you." She ran over, and they gave each other a big bear hug.

"This place isn't half-bad," he said, obviously surprised.

"What do you mean, it isn't half-bad? I have turned a broken-down shack of a place into a palace . . . with my own two hands. Come on. I'll show you around paradise." She took hold of his hand to lead him toward the house. "Oh, you didn't happen to see a goat wandering about as you drove in from town?"

"A goat?"

"No, I guess not." She grinned as his expression changed from surprise to disbelief. "Sam will probably find old Calhoun down at one of the barns. Either that goat thinks he's a cow, or he's got a crush on one of the heifers."

"Jo, Jo. Slow down. I just drove all morning to get here, and you're throwing palaces and goats at me before I catch my breath. I'm still in shock at the sight of you."

"Oh . . . right. I know I look a mess . . ."

"Joanna, who are you kidding? You look a hell of lot different from that slick city sophisticate I vaguely remember working for, but you look fabulous. Granted, the outfit didn't come off the racks at Bloomie's and your fingernails have seen better days," he said, lifting her hand up for survey, "but you are positively glowing with health from tip to toe." He did falter when his eyes rested on the work shoes, but when he met

120

her eyes again, there was no doubt his compliments were meant sincerely.

"Thanks, Gary. I feel terrific. The great outdoors really can do wonders for the body and the spirit."

"So the pioneering life turned out to be all you had dreamed," he said, a note of disappointment in his voice. "I have to admit, Jo, I kept hoping for a few smoke signals."

"I almost sent up more than a few. Every time disaster strikes I start rubbing two sticks together, but I usually give up before the fire erupts. Then I pull myself up by my bootstraps and somehow manage to get through the rough days. In fact, this morning I was tugging away on those straps like crazy. My electricity is on the fritz, my fence is down, and Calhoun has run away from home."

"I can't do much about Calhoun or your electricity, but I can pitch in on that fence."

Joanna glanced at him suspiciously. "You didn't show up here to mend fences, Gary Simms. Come inside. I'll make us some coffee, and you can tell me what it's all about."

"I see the country hasn't muddled that sharp little mind of yours, Jo."

She could see Gary really was impressed when she took him inside the house. Over the winter months she had spent a lot of time painting the place, furnishing it with some antiques picked up inexpensively at local auctions, even hanging a few of her own watercolors of the local countryside.

"I'm thinking seriously about putting up an addition off the back: a solar greenhouse to capture the heat so I wouldn't be entirely dependent on wood for the winter."

Gary studied her thoughtfully. "Next winter?"

"It's still in the thinking stage," she said, turning on the heat under the coffeepot.

"I'm having a hard time taking this all in. I guess I never really believed you'd last a few months here, never mind that you'd seriously think about staying another winter."

"I'm thinking about more than next winter, Gary. I'm considering a—a permanent move."

Gary came over to the sink to stand beside her. "Are you serious, Jo?"

"I'm in love with the dairy farmer up the dirt road," she answered with an impish grin.

Gary broke up in laughter. "You're pulling my leg . . . about all this. Right?"

"Wrong. I'm dead serious. I wrote you about Sam Chase."

"You wrote me about some neighborly farmer and his cute daughter."

"Well, he's been more than neighborly."

"You're going to marry him?"

Joanna heard the familiar sound of a pickup truck outside. She ran to the window.

"Sam found Calhoun." She waved to him from the window. "Where was he?" she called.

"Having breakfast with my cows," Sam called back, lifting the goat in his arms and setting him

122

down on the ground. "I'd better tie him up to a tree out back until you get that fence secured."

"Thanks. Come inside afterward, and meet an old friend of mine."

Joanna watched Sam from the window for a minute. Curious, Gary came over and watched with her.

"So that's your dairy farmer," he said.

Joanna grinned. "You were the one who always told me I needed the right man." Her smile faded. "The only problem is I wasn't planning on finding him here."

"You really are serious about this guy." He put his arm affectionately around her. "You know, things might feel different to you once you were back in the city, Jo. This whole experience, Sam included, could turn into a fond memory for your scrapbook."

"Don't think that possibility has never crossed my mind. I'm not sure I want to find out if it's true. So much has happened to me since I've been living here, Gary. I don't think I could begin to explain the changes I've gone through. It's not only my feelings for Sam but the way I've changed inside myself. The whole thing was such a crazy fantasy when I started out. I guess in some ways life has been a hell of a lot tougher than I imagined, but it's also been more rewarding—rewarding in ways I never dreamed would feel so terrific."

"It sounds as if you've pretty much made your decision, Jo." He sighed.

"Give me another ten minutes, and you'll

hear about the other side of the coin." She smiled wryly.

Sam walked in the back door and headed directly over to the sink to wash up and then to pour himself some coffee. Gary noticed the proprietary way in which Sam moved about. He also noticed the tense features, his quiet, almost sullen mood as Joanna introduced the two men.

Sam was not a superstitious man by nature, but as soon as he had spotted the New York license plates on the car out front, he couldn't shake the premonition of something coming to an end.

As Sam shook Gary's hand, he mumbled, "Nice to meet you."

Gary had jumped to the conclusion that Sam was thinking Gary might be an old suitor come to town to win back his girl. Quickly he said, "My wife and I've known Jo for years. Julie wanted to come up here with me, but she's got a crummy spring cold."

"Joanna's talked about you and Julie quite often," Sam said offhandedly. "She told me you were a top-notch ad man."

Gary shook his head. "Jo's the one who's top-notch. The place isn't the same without her." He shot Joanna a meaningful glance.

There was dead silence for a few moments. Then Joanna cleared her throat. "What is it, Gary? Sam and I both have figured out there's a special reason for this impromptu visit. The suspense is killing us." She managed a smile.

Gary shrugged. "Look, I get the feeling I'm

turning into the bearer of bad tidings. It's just that . . . well, we need you, Jo. We've just landed the account of a lifetime, and we're also about to lose it. To be honest, it wasn't my idea to come begging for help. Bailey made it clear that you were the one who could pull us out of this mess, and I was the one he volunteered to forge into the wilderness and bring you back. But . . . I see that you're really happy here. You probably haven't the slightest interest in pulling Bailey and Johnson out of this disaster."

"Joanna is great in disasters," Sam said softly. He had been watching Joanna's expression the whole time Gary spoke.

"I'm out of practice with advertising disasters. In fact I've put in a lot of work and effort intentionally to forget about those ulcer-producing catastrophes."

Gary laughed. "Yeah, I sure know what you mean," he said, clutching his stomach in mock pain.

Joanna didn't laugh along. Instead, she studied Gary closely. "This isn't only Bailey and Johnson's disaster, is it?"

Gary's smile faded instantly. "I swear I didn't come up here to try to save my skin, Jo. Sure, it's my disaster, too. I'm the head of the account. But when I agreed to come, it was only to see if you'd had enough of the country life, and—and I hoped maybe you were waiting for someone to beg you to come back."

"So I wouldn't have to admit defeat and come back doing my own begging?" she asked.

"There have been times I've considered doing just that."

"A lot of times," Sam added, his eyes fixed on his empty mug of coffee.

"Less lately," Joanna said quickly, then shrugged. "And along comes a day like this, when everything seems to have gone wrong. At least Calhoun's back home." She smiled at Sam, taking his cup from his hand and walking off to the stove to pour him some more. "Can I get you another refill, Gary?"

"No, thanks."

Sam sat on the edge of the sofa. "So what's this big account you're about to lose?"

Gary looked from Sam to Jo, then back to Sam again. "D and D is coming out with a new line of perfumed soaps. They were crazy about Jo's Cinderfella campaign . . . wanted her to put her magic touch on their product. Bailey talked them into giving the agency a try *sans* Jo. But they haven't liked a single idea we've come up with. And believe me, we've come up with plenty. Personally, not tooting my own horn, I think some of our ideas were really great. But they have it in their heads that you and you alone will give their soap that special pizzazz."

"If you wow them on this soap thing, I guess that means you get your hands on a number of their other products," Sam commented.

"You're pretty savvy for a farm boy," Gary said. "I see why you've stolen Jo's heart."

"Not an easy heart to steal," Sam answered, giving Joanna a broad smile. "We did get off to a smashing start but not the kind that endears a city slicker to a cowpoke."

"Sam taught me the art of being neighborly. Sometimes it was a tough lesson to learn," Joanna said with a laugh.

"But she's a fast learner," Sam added softly.

Gary awkwardly swallowed a gulp of cold coffee. "I've got to tell you something, Sam. In all the years I've known Jo, I've never seen her look happier or more beautiful. Let's forget about my ulterior motives for this visit. I'd like to take you both out for lunch. Seems to me we have something to celebrate."

"Seems to me Joanna has a decision to make first," Sam said, his eyes darting over to her.

"D and D isn't her problem, Sam. It's mine. I only thought she might be ready to reactivate her budding ulcer. Some of us can't be happy unless we're swallowing antacid tablets half the day."

"What are you saying, Sam? You think I should consider this assignment?" Joanna asked hesitantly.

"Do you want to?"

"I don't know." She shrugged and looked over at Gary. "I have to admit that when you were talking, my mind started flooding with ideas. Perfumed soaps . . ." She laughed. "It's been awhile since I've thought of products in terms of advertising gimmicks."

"But the idea appeals to you," Sam commented in such a way Joanna wasn't sure whether it was a question or a statement. And while his words weren't exactly hostile, his voice was tightly controlled. He turned away from her and moved to look out the back window, where Calhoun nibbled on grass.

Joanna could feel her anger start to surface. "It does have some appealing aspects," she said to his back.

He nodded, still facing the window.

So now he was going to play the strong, silent type, was he? "Look, Sam, if you have something to say, then say it. I don't know why you're so irritated. All I said is that—"

He turned his head, giving her a probing look over his shoulder. "It isn't what you said. It's what's spinning around right now in that gimmick-hungry mind of yours. If you want to go back, than don't hedge around about it. Tell Gary you want it, straight out."

"Who said . . . oh, excuse me. I forgot you've become a mind reader now."

"You make it easy."

Gary interrupted. "Look, you two. I didn't mean to start World War Three. The deadline we're working with comes up at the end of the month. If you aren't ready to come back permanently, you could sign on just for the next three or four weeks. Jo, I'm not pushing you, but I'm also not going to lie to you. We could use you. Don't get me wrong. Bailey and Johnson won't fold if this doesn't work out. And I'm not going to be out of a job if I don't pull this off. I've been doing great with the other accounts. If you really want no part of it, if advertising has completely soured for you, then let me buy you that lunch, give you my blessings, and return to the rat race I love, antacid tablets and all. But if you're looking for a place to use those ideas that are flooding your mind, I know just the spot."

"She needs to do it, all right," Sam said emphatically. "Actually I think she should."

"Whether I decide to do it or not, Sam Chase, it won't be because you've already made the decision. I happen to have a lot of new projects under way here," she said, turning to Gary now. "This is a busy season, Gary. I'm starting my garden; I have to fix that damn fence Calhoun busted; I was planning on staining the shingles." She sighed, turning back to Sam. "I feel you're shoving me out the door. I don't like being pushed, and I don't like the feeling that this is some kind of test."

Gary mumbled something about stepping outside for a few minutes. Neither of them paid attention when he left.

"I don't like never knowing for sure where you really feel you belong." Sam came up to her. "In fact, I don't like this whole thing . . . not one bit. But there's no point in either of us denying deep down you really want to go. Right?"

"What if you come with me, Sam? It's only for a few weeks. We could take Penelope, too. You could show her the sights during the day while I was working. Who knows? Maybe you'll like the experience," she said.

"I don't. I spent six years in New York City, Jo. Four years at Columbia University and two years working for a large import-export company. I had the experience of city life. I also had my fill of it. When I came up to Brandon, I knew I'd found what I wanted . . . without a doubt . . . without any misgivings. I know what I want now, too," he said, inhaling slowly, his features hardening to a cool, angry set. "I should have known better than to let myself believe that you were starting to feel you belonged in Brandon, that you could give up your old life for something new, something you'd found that was more important."

Joanna started to protest, but Sam held up his hand, his expression softening. "Don't argue with me, Jo. I'm telling you to go because I know you'll end up going anyway. If I tried to fight it, I might end up losing you. I guess that could still happen, and that's what hurts. I don't like feeling helpless, and I'd better warn you I'm a lousy loser. But we've come this far . . ." His voice trailed off. He looked back out the window and watched Gary walk over to the goat and pat him gingerly. A fleeting smile touched his face.

"Why don't you go out with Gary for lunch? You probably have a lot to discuss. I need to get back to the farm. I'll see you tonight," he said, his voice edged with resignation.

He bent to kiss her, even though they both felt angry and hurt. Joanna turned her face to the side so that his lips landed on her cheek. He laughed softly and gripped her by the shoulders.

"Let's try again." Before she could argue, he pulled her to him to kiss her passionately. "This is what's waiting for you when you come back," he whispered in her ear.

"I wish Gary hadn't shown up." She sighed.

"Me, too. But we have to deal with it, haven't we?" He kissed her again, briefly this time, and let go of her, then tapped on the window, waved good-bye to Gary, and headed toward the front door.

"Have a nice lunch," he said casually, forcing a weak smile as he walked outside.

Joanna stood in the middle of the room, swallowing hard to stave off tears. She couldn't decide if she was sad, angry, or scared. And she'd thought the day had *begun* badly!

Once Sam had climbed into the cabin of his truck, all the remnants of his defenses melted. He didn't want her to leave. He was as scared as she was that she wouldn't return. And he could feel his anger starting to get the best of him. Damn it, he was in love with her. He wanted nothing more than to hear her tell Gary Simms she wouldn't return to that ad agency—for three weeks or three minutes. But she hadn't been able to say that. And Sam couldn't pretend her ambivalence was linked solely to an allegiance to Gary. She wasn't thinking only about her friend or about her old ties to Bailey and Johnson.

He had wanted more than anything to tell her to stay. Instead he had done just the opposite, knowing it was his only choice, knowing that he could lose her either way.

Driving slowly back to the farm, he consoled

himself with the knowledge that he had a few important factors in his favor. He had a pretty strong hunch that if Joanna left, she would miss him, Penelope, and old Calhoun more than she herself might realize.

All the months it had taken Joanna to win over Carol Maddox at the Pine Tree Inn went down the drain when she walked in with Gary Simms. Carol eyed them with a cool, detached expression, one Joanna knew well. She was sure Carol interpreted this luncheon date as a clear act of betrayal of Sam, especially when Gary put his arm around her as they walked across the dining room to their table.

Joanna nudged Gary, whispering, "Watch yourself, Simms. I'm a country girl who has to watch her reputation. This little stroll through the restaurant will keep the locals buzzing for weeks."

"Shall I pull out some wedding pictures of me and Julie?" he asked.

"No, that would be worse. Then they'd all think I was a home wrecker as well as cheating on their favorite farmer."

When they sat down at a small window table, Gary said, "He seems like a nice guy. Bright, too."

Joanna grinned. "He alternates between *The Farmer's Almanac* and *The Wall Street Journal*. Funny he'd never told me until today he'd gone to school and worked in New York."

"It might have been a period in his life he'd

132

just as soon forget about. Or maybe he avoided talking about it so he wouldn't be influencing you unfairly. He seems big on wanting you to make up your own mind."

Joanna sighed. "I guess I was hoping to hear him say he didn't want me to go, that he wasn't willing to risk losing me to 'urban renewal.'" She had to pause at that thought. "Then you could have challenged him to a duel to see who was going to win the little lady in the steel-tipped shoes: the love of her life or Bailey and Johnson? Would the prize be a simple gold band or a year's supply of sweet-smelling soap? And talking about soap . . ."

"Why don't I feel great about the duel I seem to have just won?"

"I don't feel great either," Joanna admitted, "but if Sam wants me to take that test, that's what I am going to do. Lather away," she said with a sigh, giving Gary a familiar look that signaled: Let's get down to the business at hand.

Gary smiled. "You can take the girl out of the city, but you can't take the city out of the girl."

"That saying does not fill me with good cheer, but I'm afraid it may be true nonetheless."

They discussed soap throughout lunch, Joanna's head swimming with ideas. By the time they finished eating she couldn't deny that tackling this project had her energized.

"I have to admit you were right, Sam. I should go back. This is a perfect way to see . . . I mean, it's only one campaign. I'll be done with it

133

in a few weeks. This will give me a chance to visit friends, do some shopping, see a play or two on Broadway." She stopped talking, conscious of his silent appraisal. "Why are you sulking? This was your idea."

"I'm not sulking. And it wasn't my idea. I just offered an opinion."

"Was that what it was? An opinion?"

"What are you ticked off about? Since I came over, you've been walking on cloud nine about this whole thing. Go on. Tell me you haven't had one thought about—about soap since you had lunch with Gary Simms."

"Of course, I've been thinking about a campaign pitch for that soap. And okay, I'm excited about some of the ideas that are floating around my head. It's—it's a pleasant change, if you want to know the truth, from worrying about clogged fuel lines, runaway goats, seedlings that continually get crushed by my pale green thumb. A thumb, now that I think about it, that hasn't had a manicure in almost seven months. Well, Mr. Chase, I plan to treat all ten of my fingers to luxury over the next few weeks. I'm going to wine them and dine them. And I'm going to get my hair cut by someone who doesn't use the same shears he uses on my locks to trim his—his sheep when he closes the barbershop for the night. I am going to walk into a restaurant without a single thought in my mind about having to force the special of the day down my throat so the cook's feelings won't be hurt and so his wife will smile and say hello to me the next time I walk in. I am going to buy myself a pair of the highest-heeled sandals I can find, even if they aren't in style right now, and I won't complain even once about aching feet . . . or aching anything, for that matter. Believe me, in the past few months this body of mine has ached enough for a lifetime." She paused to catch her breath, trying to think of something else to say.

"Are you finished?" he snapped.

"No. Just give me a minute. I'm sure there's more."

"I've heard enough to get the picture." He turned to leave.

"Where are you going?"

"I'm going home, Jo."

"Sam."

"You've made your point."

She walked over to him. Staring down at her cracked fingernails, she said hesitantly, "I may have overstated it."

"I'd better leave before I start overstating some of mine," he said in that tight, controlled way that was becoming all too familiar to Joanna.

He headed for the door, but Joanna grabbed his sleeve. "Sam, we're two adults. Why can't we behave rationally about this whole thing?"

Sam presented her with one of his inscrutable smiles. "And all this time I thought I was presenting myself at my rational best."

He glanced down at his sleeve. Joanna's fingers still gripped the material tightly. She mumbled something under her breath, dropped her hand, and turned her back.

She missed seeing the pained look in Sam's eyes as he studied her for a brief moment before stepping out the door.

CHAPTER EIGHT

Joanna was in a frenzy for the next two days, getting her house in order for her departure. Gary had called her from New York the day before to say that everyone at the agency was ecstatic about her return. Joanna was quick to reiterate that this was more a brief consultation than a return to Bailey and Johnson. Even though Gary had hastily reassured her that was understood by all, Joanna had a suspicion he wasn't fully buying her avowal to make this re-entry short and sweet.

"Okay, Calhoun," Joanna cooed as she fed him a few alfalfa pellets, "you be a good little goat now. I'll be home soon. And don't you worry for one minute about winding up adopted."

She stared at the goat as he wandered away from the fence to a pile of rocks she had so carefully arranged to provide him with exercise and amusement.

"You probably wouldn't mind being adopted by Sam at that," she said out loud with a sigh. "You'd have a grand old time romping around the farm. Penelope and Sam would see to it that you were happy."

She gathered up her sledgehammer, gave the mended fence one last good shake, and smiled with satisfaction. Calhoun would have his work cut out for him if he were going to make his way through this enclosure.

Returning to the house, Joanna mentally ran through the checklist of what was still left to be done. There'd been a fierce intensity about her need to be organized these past couple of days. Why couldn't she shake this sense of time running out? She looked about the cabin. Her eyes then wandered out the window to her newly turned garden. She had accomplished a lot, but nothing was finished. Nothing ever was truly completed up here. Instead, life moved in cycles. In those first months Joanna had been too used to the concept of beginnings and endings —in work and in relationships—to be willing to pace herself so she could meet the constant demands that altered but never stopped. Time and exhaustion had been her best teachers.

No, she thought, a sharp knot wrenching her stomach, Sam had been the best teacher. He had taught her much about life in the country. He had also taught her much about love. And she still had more to learn. But Gary's arrival had broken the cycle of her life in Brandon, and his presence had generated confusion and doubts. No matter how hard Joanna fought against it, her mind had begun recounting some of the hardships and disadvantages of her rugged rural life. She countered with all the pluses, but somehow the pros seemed weak, measured against the cons.

Her thoughts always returned to Sam and her one sure belief: that she loved him and he loved her. It overrode many of her doubts—or at least up until the moment she knew she wanted to take on that soap account. She had tried to make Sam believe his shove was responsible for her decision, but that wasn't true. She wanted to take on this challenge, even though the risks it brought scared the hell out of her.

Joanna was cleaning out her refrigerator when she heard a light rap on her front door. It opened before she called out.

"Hi, Penelope." Joanna looked over her shoulder, Tupperware container in her hand. "I thought I heard the school bus pull up."

"Do you need some help . . . getting ready?" Penelope dropped her school bag near the door and walked over to the kitchen area. "That smells awful," she said, scrunching her nose. "What is it?"

"That's what I'm trying to remember," Joanna answered with a grin. "I think this is my attempt at pickling zucchinis. I'm not sure whether those green things are the vegetable or whether I've discovered the mold that will cure a rare disease."

"I vote for the mold."

"I vote for tossing it out," Joanna said, dumping the contents into the plastic trash bag. "Sam would probably tell me it was perfect for my mulch pile, but I've finished mulching for this season." She continued pulling items from the refrigerator as she talked, most of them going into the garbage.

"What about these dinner rolls? They're the ones we made together the other day. Do you want to take them home?"

Penelope shook her head slowly. "No, thanks." She wandered over to one of the opened cupboards. "Are you emptying everything out?"

Joanna was struck by the note of concern in Penelope's voice and the sad expression on her face. She stood up, closed the refrigerator door, and walked toward her young friend, a gentle smile on her face.

"I thought I'd use my trip back to the city for a few weeks as a good excuse to do my spring cleaning. Going through all my cupboards and the fridge is my least favorite chore. Now I'm forced to face it, or I might return to find some four-legged tenants inhabiting my happy home." She put her arm lightly around Penelope's shoulder. "I could use some help in the bedroom."

Penelope nodded. They walked together into the small room, where Joanna had already begun packing her suitcase.

"Sam has sure been in a lousy mood since the other day," Penelope said abruptly while Joanna folded a shirt.

"Has he?"

140

"I don't think he really wants you to go to New York."

"How do you feel about my going?"

Penelope grinned impishly. "Maybe you'll finally check out the Statue of Liberty." Her smile faded. "I don't mind about your going as long as you really are coming back."

"I am, Penelope."

"Well, I guess I was wondering on account of . . . you seem to be taking an awful lot of stuff back with you."

Joanna saw Penelope's eyes drift to the almost empty closet. "I don't have very much here to begin with. And I'll need these casual things to wear when I'm not at work." She pointed down to the foot of her bed. "I'm leaving my work shoes here. That's a sure sign I'm coming back. They're my most treasured possessions." She jabbed Penelope playfully in the shoulder.

"Sam isn't talking about it, but I'll bet he wants to marry you, Jo." Penelope idly folded up a sweater as she spoke. "Do you want to marry him?"

"You've decided to take on the role of Cupid," Joanna commented softly.

"I just figured that if the two of you got yourselves engaged and all, Sam wouldn't be so uptight. He'd know you'd come back . . . if there was something official. You know what I mean."

Joanna sat beside Penelope on the bed. "Neither of us is ready to take that step yet, Penelope. We are thinking about it . . . very

141

seriously. A decision as important as getting married deserves very careful consideration."

"Are you worried because of me? I mean, it couldn't be too big a thrill getting saddled with a fifteen- almost sixteen-year-old daughter right when you got married. You'll probably want kids of your own . . . and maybe a husband who doesn't already have any. Let's face it . . . I could get in the way."

Joanna reached out and took Penelope's hand. "You would never be in the way. And I'm not worried—" She took a slow, deep breath, then looked directly into Penelope's eyes. "No. That's not true. I care too much about our relationship to pretend I have no fears or concerns. But it isn't the way you think." She sighed, a wistful smile on her face. "When I first moved in here, I felt completely inept. I didn't know the first thing about coping with the new life-style I had so impulsively decided was essential to my sanity. In fact, more than a few times I thought I'd go nuts trying to struggle through one more day. Let me tell you, I cried myself to sleep quite a few nights at first. Then, little by little, I learned the basics of survival."

"I think you've done great. You can handle pretty much anything you set out to do."

"I guess that's one of the things that worries me about marrying your dad. Learning how to fix up a house, plant a garden, put up a fence—that's a long way from learning to be a wife and mother . . ."

"Both at the same time," Penelope tacked on.

"Right," Joanna said. "You and Sam have gotten along terrifically up to now. That's part of my concern. I don't honestly know how I could fit in; I'm not sure it would work out."

"Are you afraid I'll be jealous?"

"Would you be?"

"Sure, a little . . . sometimes. But I'd also be happy a lot of times. I wouldn't feel so lonely if you were around more. And it's not always so easy talking things over with Sam . . . you know what I mean. I'm growing up. Which is another thing—what's going to happen to Sam when I go off to college or get a job? He'll be all alone."

"Maybe he wouldn't mind that," Joanna pointed out.

"Do you mind being alone?" Penelope asked bluntly.

Joanna shrugged. "Sometimes. More since I met Sam. Penelope, I don't want you to think that you are the main reason I haven't been able to decide about getting married."

"You mean you don't know if you really want to live up here permanently. I know Sam still thinks you like the city more. Or that you will, once you go back. That's what he thought when you first came, and now I think he's feeling that way again."

"I'm sure he is concerned. That's one reason why I'm going back: to find out if he's right or not."

"Deep down I wish you weren't going. Oh, I know there's probably a lot of exciting things to do and see in the city, but you have lots to do here, too. There're all the things you want to work on in the house, and there's your garden. You'll miss seeing all the vegetables start to grow. And what about poor Calhoun? He's going to miss you like crazy. I—I even talked with a kid at school whose father sells chickens. You always said one of these days you'd buy some. Oh, Jo, I'm going to miss you. I won't be able to stop over after school, to tell you all the things I don't tell anyone else. We won't be baking bread together or—or planning the new shed for Calhoun . . . or talking about who's going to ask me to the school dance . . . or . . ." Tears streamed down her cheeks, and the words choked in her throat.

Joanna couldn't talk either. Her own tears flowed freely. Why was she leaving everything that mattered, the people she loved most? She had a sudden impulse to rush to the phone, call Gary, and tell him to forget their agreement. Right now the last thing in the world she wanted to do was board that 5:00 P.M. Greyhound bus for New York City.

"I guess I'm being silly," Penelope said finally, gulping back the tears. "You'll be back in a few weeks, like you said."

"Right." Joanna nodded, wiping her wet cheeks.

They heard footsteps crossing the living room. Both looked up to see Sam standing in the doorway of the bedroom.

"Is this a private farewell party, or am I invited?" he asked, watching them both furiously brush away their tears.

"It's open house," Joanna answered, her embarrassment obvious. "Pull out a hankie and join us."

"I left my hankie home," he rasped. "But it is a touching scene."

Penelope took one look at her father's smoldering expression and placed the half-folded sweater she'd been holding this whole time into Joanna's suitcase.

"I have to get home and do some schoolwork." She looked straight at Joanna, giving her a "buck up, kid" kind of smile. "See you in a few weeks. Give my love to Miss Liberty if you get the chance to visit her." She attempted a grin, her eyes still misty.

"Keep an eye on my garden . . . and Calhoun. Don't go spoiling him so he's impossible when I get back. And—and find out how much that guy wants for his chickens."

Penelope nodded, hurrying out as the tears started down her cheek again.

"Chickens?" Sam asked, sitting next to Joanna on the bed.

"Didn't I ever tell you about my uncle the chicken farmer?" She laughed hesitantly, the sound fading fast when he didn't offer so much as the glimmer of a smile.

"Sam, what am I doing this for? I'm not even sure I want to go to New York."

He walked around the room, observing, as his daughter had earlier, that Joanna had cleaned out most of her belongings. Idly he swung the closet door back and forth, and a high-pitched noise from the hinges was the only sound other than their breathing.

"I'll have to take care of that squeak when I get back," Joanna muttered. If she'd had any hopes that they were going to reach some kind of rapprochement before she left, those hopes were dimming rapidly.

"That should be a pretty exciting task," Sam observed, his stroll around the room turning into more of a pacing.

Joanna put a few sweaters in the suitcase, trying to ignore the steady rhythm of his footsteps. "I've given this whole decision a lot of thought, Sam," she said with as calm a voice as she could muster, "and I think I have things in a clearer perspective now."

Sam drew closer, his footsteps coming to an abrupt halt a few inches from her. "That's great, Jo. I'd love to hear all about it. Matter of fact, I've been doing a lot of thinking these past couple of days myself. Got some . . . perspective on it all, too. Something tells me our . . . perspectives might be different."

Joanna glanced up at him, shaking her head. "Look, Sam, I don't want to go off angry. Maybe we ought to table this discussion before we start—"

"Before we start . . . what?" he snapped. "Telling the truth? Let me tell you the truth, as I see it. You had yourself a grand old time playing little Miss Country Gal . . . and messing up a

146

couple of other people's lives—like Penelope's and mine—in the process." He grabbed hold of her shoulders, his eyes boring down on her.

"Sam, stop. You're hurting me, and—and you're behaving completely irrationally."

"Oh, right. We're supposed to be two rational people," he said sarcastically, his fingers still maintaining a firm grip. "Let's be nice and civilized, right? You had your little experiment in country living, and now it's time to go home. I suppose I should give you a fond, loving farewell and nurse my bruises in private. That would be civilized, wouldn't it? That must be the way it's done in the big city."

"This isn't like you, Sam. You—you said you understood."

He didn't seem to hear her. "That's not the way it's done up here, Jo. I told you way back that I take my romancing seriously. You want to play games, you found yourself the wrong partner. I don't want games, experiments, people I love popping in and out of my life because they have to find themselves. You want to know what I think?" He glared at her as he spoke.

"No," she said.

"Well, I'm going to tell you anyway. You're so busy trying to find yourself that you're walking out on the one place it's really happening for you. But you can't see that, can you? No, you're too devoted to the search. All part of the game, I suppose."

"I'm playing games, am I?" she snapped, struggling to loosen his grip to no avail. "Let go

147

of me, damn it. You're the one playing games—word games. With a little brawn thrown in. Take your hands off me, Sam. I'm not participating in this adolescent show of hurt pride. I never promised I wouldn't go back—"

"No," he cut in, "you didn't promise." He laughed, but there was no mirth in the sound. "I guess I was naïve enough to think that our becoming lovers implied some kind of a commitment on your part. But then I'm just a down-home country boy. I'd better go read some of Penelope's *Ms* magazines to find out what the new woman is all about."

"Maybe you should," she replied. "It might offset the macho he-man junk you obviously identify with."

He dropped his hands and took a couple of steps back.

She sighed, rubbing her shoulder. "I thought the other day you were at least making some effort to understand." Her voice broke. "I still have some packing to do," she managed to say.

"The problem is, I do understand." After he'd let go of her arm, they had stayed frozen in position. Now Sam shrugged, his gaze sweeping the room. "I guess you'd better get finished here if you plan to make your bus."

Joanna felt as if a large chunk of her life were slipping out of her fingers. Making two tight fists against her sides didn't help. "We need to talk this out, Sam. I—I could take a later bus."

He shook his head. "Talking isn't going to change anything. We both have our feelings

. . . and I guess we'll each have to work them through in our own way."

Joanna stared at him in despair. She could forget this whole crazy business, run into his arms, and tell him she didn't want to go. But that wasn't true. She had to go back to her old world, taste it once more . . . to be sure. And standing here with Sam in this silent face-off, she knew the real issue was whether she would actually come back. Sam mattered more to her than she'd ever realized. But he wanted commitment. Her decision to go back to New York was clearly a statement as loud as any verbal one she could make that she wasn't ready. Not yet. She wanted to be as ready as Sam was; she wanted to make him understand that she was testing herself in this way because their relationship was so important to her. But he had abandoned his willingness to be reasonable. He was hurt. And she understood—but that wasn't helping them feel closer.

"I'll call you from the city."

"No."

"Sam, don't just shut me off. We—we do have something special together. Don't destroy it now," she pleaded, all of her own anger drained. In its place sat cold fear. She didn't want to lose him. "I'm coming back, Sam. When I do, it will be for good. I truly believe that."

"We'll talk then." For a brief moment there was a hint of warmth in his expression, but it disappeared so quickly Joanna couldn't be sure she hadn't just imagined it. What she saw on his face before he walked out the door was only a look of weary resignation.

She sat back down on her bed, staring disconsolately at her suitcase. She'd felt better with Sam's rage than with his chilling acquiescence. Against anger she could fight back, but the fight seemed to be knocked out of her. She reached out and closed the suitcase. There was no turning back now.

Sam drove his pickup over the gravel road so fast that several times his head made sharp contact with the roof of the cabin. He seemed not to notice. He went straight down to the dairy, where Penelope was doing some chores. Sam's foreman and three farmhands were also hard at work. Sam managed to chew out everyone in sight—so unlike him no one seemed sure how to react. After a while he stormed off, leaving the group staring at each other in amazement.

"What was all that about?"

"Beats me."

"I never saw Sam Chase that mad in all the years I've worked for him. Except maybe the day those teen-agers stole off with two of his prize calves as a prank."

Penelope leaned her broom against the wall and joined the others. She gave them a broad, knowing grin. "This time it's worse. He's in love."

The bus grunted, jerked, and slowly pulled out into the street. Joanna sat at the window, staring out at the little town of Brandon. One or two people waved, and Joanna managed a small smile despite the tears trickling down her cheek. She knew better than to hope Sam would magically appear to see her off. After their last conversation she wasn't even sure he'd be waiting for her when she returned. *If she returned*, a small, unbidden voice whispered.

There was so much here to come back for, she thought, smiling through her tears. But as the bus pulled onto the highway, the tiny Vermont town disappearing from view, Joanna knew that returning would take even more of a commitment than staying would have required. Once again she was overwhelmed by the sense of being caught between two uniquely different worlds, each of which she had come to know intimately, each of which offered her something she wanted.

She arrived in New York at 9:00 P.M. She had called Gary before she'd boarded the bus to tell him not to bother picking her up. She'd go to a hotel for the night and see him at the office the next morning.

She was amazed at the culture shock she was experiencing as she stood on the crowded street in front of the bus terminal, competing with at least eight other people for a taxi. She certainly hadn't been gone that long, yet the noises, the traffic, the crowded streets all felt a little alien.

Adjusting quickly, Joanna darted out into the street to grab a cab, beating out the other eight people. *Always take the offense,* she said to herself with a smile, settling into the cab, an airconditioned one at that.

After a quick meal in the restaurant of the Gramercy Park Hotel she went up to her room. Sinking onto the bed, relieved that the mattress was nice and firm, she closed her eyes for a brief time. Thoughts of Sam prevented her from dozing off. She stared at the telephone and held a brief debate with herself. She wanted to hear his voice. She wanted to tell him that she missed him already. She wanted to make him believe that in a few weeks she would be back in his arms.

"Hi, Sam." She held the phone so close to her lips that her voice sounded muffled, and at first Sam didn't recognize it. "It's me. Jo."

"Are you calling from your cabin?"

"Of course not. I'm in New York. At the Gramercy—"

"I thought we went through that, Jo. I told you not to call from the city." He spoke so sharply Joanna pulled the phone away from her ear.

"Sam, this is ridiculous. I know you said—"

"I meant it, Jo. You seem to have trouble realizing that I do mean what I say. I don't bounce back and forth like some damn volleyball."

"Is that how you see it? Well, I may be a—a volleyball, but you are a stubborn, unreasonable, irrational steel rod. Not only do you not bounce, but you can't even bend an inch. When you're ready to give a little—a fraction will do—

then you can call me. Because you damn well won't have to worry about my phoning you again."

She slammed the phone down before Sam could respond. Not that she thought he would offer much of a response anyway. That man was more stubborn than Calhoun.

After the call she felt better, though. He had been unyielding on the phone, but she could hear those sparks of anger flying across the line. He cared; he really cared. He might even call once he had simmered down a little. She took that thought back to bed with her. It was only a little after ten, but she'd had one hell of a day, and exhaustion now washed over her. She fell asleep easily.

Sam didn't sleep well at all. He finally got into bed around midnight, knowing even if he managed any sleep, he'd be wiped out all the next day. The alarm was set for five. He toyed with the notion of moving the hour hand ahead to six, but he decided it wouldn't help much.

Loneliness replaced his anger. After Joanna had hung up on him, he was able to keep his fury brewing for another hour or two. But as time passed, a feeling of emptiness intruded. He told himself he was justified in his anger. She had no business letting him believe she was really content with her life here, content with him. He had been planning to ask her to marry him when he stormed into her cabin this afternoon.

Until he saw the empty closet, Joanna's and

153

Penelope's tear-streaked faces, the open suitcase. She was leaving. That was that.

He didn't blow up often. Usually, if he allowed himself a little time to sort things out, he came to the decision that whatever had ticked him off wasn't worth going crazy over.

Joanna was worth it. He wasn't able to sort out his feelings reasonably where she was concerned. They just seemed to erupt, overwhelming him. He was angry at her for leaving him, angry at himself for getting involved with her in the first place when that little voice in his head had warned him regularly to keep his distance. He hadn't wanted a brief, magical affair, an experiment in caring. A few months ago he might have been able to let her go rationally and objectively. Now he was poised between fury and fear. He couldn't shake the thought that she was going to be swallowed up by New York, by the ad agency, by the hectic, exciting fast pace of city life.

She'd stood in front of the cabin that first day looking as if she'd just stepped out of *Town and Country* magazine. They were last year's designer jeans, she'd said indignantly, hacking away at her closet door with that saw. He'd been sure she'd fly the coop before the week was up.

The longer she stayed in Brandon, the more he'd let himself believe it could be permanent. He loved her fierce determination to gain mastery, her persistence and stamina. He loved her. But he told himself he wouldn't call. Not because, as Joanna had accused him, he was being wholly inflexible but because he was lousy at playing volleyball. Especially when he was worried about losing.

CHAPTER NINE

"I think we're beginning to get somewhere, Jo. Hopkins was actually smiling when he walked out of the meeting." Tom Bailey adjusted his tie, the strain behind his brown eyes fading. He swept his hand across the polished mahogany conference table. Joanna was familiar with the gesture. It signified that matters were going to work out smoothly.

"If that scrunched-up crease across Hopkins's mouth was a smile, I'd hate to see him unhappy," Joanna replied, gathering the storyboards for the television ads into her large portfolio case.

"Believe me, when he's not pleased, he's quite another sight. Fortunately for all of us, you've brought the sunshine into his face . . . as well as come across with some absolutely fabulous ideas."

"I have to admit I'm impressing myself. Butterflies were gathering for a major convention in the pit of my stomach when I walked through those swinging glass doors two weeks ago. I was afraid my creative mind had turned to chopped liver, that the wheels had stopped turning." Joanna stretched, a contented smile relaxing her features. They had just come through a pressure-filled meeting. There hadn't been a relaxed muscle in the room for the past hour and a half. Now, with Hopkins's guarded approval, Joanna had a direction to follow that could make this campaign a smash success.

"I'm very excited, Jo. I don't need to tell you what this account could do for this agency . . . or for you," Tom tacked on softly.

Her contented smile faded. In a voice more hesitant than she would admit she felt, she said, "This was a one-shot deal, Tom."

"Jo, come on. I see that old sparkle back in your eyes, the look of pride when Hopkins told you he liked the way you think. You've been bursting with energy and creative ideas since you came back. And just look at you, Jo. Hair all done up by some hotshot stylist on Fifth Avenue, a dress that's either a designer's original or a terrific copy. Honey, you've got New York written all over you. Sure, country life obviously agreed with you. Giving yourself a little time off, getting out of the rat race—that had a nice, mellowing effect. You're more relaxed now. Nothing seems to throw you. With that attitude you could take the advertising world by storm."

"Tom, please. I don't want to go into all this now. You're catching me at a vulnerable time. I've just gotten a large sampling of success, and I'm afraid some of it has gone to my head. So don't start sweet-talking me about the joys of the advertising world. Those Rolaids are still sitting in the bottom of my purse, even if I haven't had to reach for any yet. It's only a matter of time." Her look was beseeching, but her speech lacked conviction. She found herself wishing everything hadn't gone so smoothly for the past two weeks.

Fourteen days of theater, art galleries, shopping, visiting friends, working in a nurturing environment where everyone seemed thrilled to see her again—all of it had left Joanna confused and disoriented. Even the morning rush hour was a novelty after all those months. Where was the old outrage at being cramped like a sardine into an already overflowing can? She hadn't even received a surreptitious pinch from the sleazy-looking guy hanging onto the subway strap next to hers, nothing to get her old ire going again.

Since her apartment was still being sublet, the ad agency was footing the bill for an attractive furnished studio a short distance from Central Park. Instead of a sky blue air shaft view, Joanna could actually see a smattering of real live trees from her casement window.

The first night in her apartment she had soaked so long in her bubble-filled bathtub she could easily have been mistaken for a well-dried prune when she finally stepped out. And it had felt heavenly. The dishwasher, the apartment-size washer and dryer neatly stacked in the closet off the kitchen, and the endless hot-water supply—all contributed to her luxurious comfort . . . and incredible guilt. What had become of her rugged spirit, her drive and determination not only to rough it in the wilderness but also to love every minute of the struggle?

The crazy part was that she *had* loved it. And even as she flicked on the various switches that made the modern woman's life a veritable dream, she missed the water heater that continually acted up, the broken-down pickup truck that always needed another new part. She missed the fresh mountain air, the sight of a sky that wasn't blocked out by hundreds of towering buildings hogging the light and the sun. She missed chatting with Bob Webster down at the hardware store about her latest do-it-yourself project. She hoped Craig Simon had asked Penelope to the dance for next Saturday. Most of all, she missed Sam . . . missed him so much that she kept having to fight the temptation to call him again, even though she'd vowed she wouldn't.

What would she say if she did break her vow? She didn't know. That, she realized, was the real reason she hadn't tried to break through Sam's stubborn refusal to talk reasonably. The problem was that no matter how much she missed her life in Brandon, the excitement, the stimulation, the activity, and even the tensions and the crowds of the city held a special enchantment for her. That enchantment would come through in her conversation with Sam despite any efforts she might make to conceal it.

Nights Joanna found herself agonizing over

159

what she really wanted out of her life. Back in Brandon waited the man of her dreams, a man who loved her and made her feel fantastically happy. Here in New York her career had never looked brighter than it did at this very moment. Tom Bailey was not blowing hot air when he implied this account could bring her a little fame and fortune.

After her talk with Tom, Joanna bumped into Gary Simms as she returned to her office. He was halfway out her door.

"Oh, good. I was looking for you." He greeted her with a broad grin. "Nice work this morning, Miss Winfield."

"I know. I know. I put an excuse for a smile on Hopkins's plump mug. If you want to hear the truth, Gary, it is not the biggest thrill of a life-time," she snapped, storming past him into her office. Gary did an about-face and followed her. He shut the door firmly behind him.

"Okay, Jo. Out with it," he ordered, grabbing her shoulders and gently nudging her into her swivel chair. "When I walked out of that meeting twenty minutes ago and left you with Tom, you looked as if you were floating somewhere in the vicinity of, if not right on, cloud nine. Don't tell me the old guy made a pass at you," he said jokingly.

"As a matter of fact, he did," she answered, giving him an angry glare. "Not at my body, but a direct attack on my mind. He wants it." She looked up at Gary, a half smile now blending with a half grimace. "He wants it badly."

"Can't say as how the old man has bad taste. Haven't I always said you had a great-looking . . . mind?"

They exchanged a smile. Gary reached over from where he was perched on the edge of her desk and took her hand. "Are you wishing I had never shown up in Shangri-la two weeks ago?"

"You're a terrific mind reader, Gary. Or else I'm wearing a large, easy-to-read sign."

"The latter," he affirmed. "In bold bloodred print. But don't worry about it. This campaign is going swimmingly. In another few weeks you can hop a bus back to the mountains. We'll all be rushing after you, trying to grab hold and keep you here with us, but you've never been a woman to let anyone or anything stop you from going after what you want."

"That's the problem. What do I want? Come on, Gary. Do some proper mind-reading. Tell me what the hell to do."

"I wish I could. Don't forget I'm the one that came upon you in Shangri-la looking like the Miss America of the great outdoors. With stars flickering in your eyes . . . no less."

"Not starry eyes, Gary. Give me a break. I'm going to reach for a Rolaids in another minute. Then again, maybe I should. That could solve all my problems."

"Lady, you've been reading too much of your own copy. No one little antacid tablet is going to work that kind of miracle."

"Yes, it will. I vowed that if I needed to chew one antacid, I was going to hightail it back to

161

Brandon as fast as the Greyhound bus would take me."

"Shall I unwrap the package?"

Joanna looked so forlorn that Gary wanted to take her in his arms and reassure her everything would work out fine. Only he had no idea it would. Any way he looked at it, Joanna was going to have to give up something she cared deeply about.

"My stomach is fine, unfortunately," she said with a smirk. "It's my head and heart that are suffering. Oh, Gary, how can it feel so good to be back here and so absolutely awful at the same time?"

"Because like all of us, Jo, you want to have your cake and eat it, too."

"Yeah, but Sam is holding the plate—and the damn utensils."

"I could introduce you to Julie's third cousin who's just settled in town. He loves New York. And I guarantee he'd positively flip over you."

"Some help you are, Gary Simms. How could you forget so soon all my fervent anti-blind-date speeches. Besides"—she closed her eyes, fighting back a sudden attack of weepiness—"I love Sam."

"Yeah, I know."

"Bailey sees big things ahead for me." She paused, her eyes drifting toward her portfolio propped against the wall. Then she turned back to Gary. "Do you realize that next Thursday at precisely eleven thirty-two P.M. I am going to bid my fond farewell to my twenties, Gary? I

162

always said that when I turned thirty, I would have my life laid out in just the right direction. Occasionally that prediction included having the right guy at my side, but given my previous doses of disappointment in that area, I focused mainly on my career. Now Bailey is more than hinting at lining my path to success in gold. A year ago I would have slipped into my Gucci pumps and headed right for that road. Now one foot is encased in Gucci leather, and the other one is tied into a well-worn steel-tipped work shoe. Don't think for a minute that it's easy to walk this way."

"I have to be honest. You look terrific in either style. The question is: Which feels more comfortable?"

"Thanks a lot, Gary. Questions I've got plenty of. It's answers I crave."

"Sorry, Jo. If answers came easy to me, I wouldn't have had to go looking for you in Shangri-la in the first place. Maybe you ought to ring up Sam and see if he can help."

"Sam has all the answers, but they don't necessarily match my questions. Besides, we've decided not to talk on the phone for a while—Sam's decision. I'm afraid I'm going to have to struggle through this thing alone, tripping over my feet in the process no doubt. I just hope I don't land face first."

Gary stared down at his shiny black matched shoes, thinking it would really be tough to be in Joanna's mismatched ones. Not only did he not have the answers for her, but he was biased toward wanting her to stay. It was good to have her back. She managed to spark creativity and energy in everyone around her. Gary was feeling back on target with this new campaign, encouraged by Joanna's bright, innovative ideas.

Joanna reached out and patted his knee affectionately. "Maybe when I actually turn thirty next week, the fairy who looks over middle-aged maidens will appear and show me the way."

"Middle-aged, my . . . arse," he said with a huge grin.

"If you throw me that line 'You're not getting older; you're getting better,' I'll personally ask Bailey to toss you out of this place on *your* well-padded arse."

"Never fear. I never spout copy or let it go to my head. Just to my bank account."

"Maybe I'm going through what *Cosmo* labels early mid-life crisis. I'd better go reread that article. If there is no such thing as a fairy godmother to guide me gently into middle age, would *Cosmo* fail me?"

"Now you've got me nervous again," he remarked. "It used to be *Ms,* and now it's *Cosmo.* There's a definite trend here. I think I hear a moo cow in the distance."

"I hear it calling to me every day. Not to mention Calhoun beckoning me home to be a proper mother again."

"Goats adjust well to foster parents. I read about that just the other day in *Field and Stream,*" Gary said jokingly.

Joanna laughed. "Since when do you read *Field and Stream?*"

"Since I switched dentists. This guy happens to be a nut for two things: fishing and preventive care for teeth. When it's a choice between *Dental News* and *Field and Stream,* I'll go with fish and deer any day."

"And goats, huh? You probably think I'm nuts that I feel homesick for a goat. But I do."

"I don't think you're nuts, Jo," he said affectionately.

"And I have such great plans for turning the old shed on my property into a first-class chicken coop."

"Now I think you're nuts." He chuckled.

"Didn't I ever tell you about my uncle the— the—" Her sobs burst out so suddenly that Joanna was as surprised as Gary. He fumbled behind him for the box of tissues and grabbed a handful, which Joanna immediately clutched to her face.

Gary attempted to comfort her by gently rubbing her back, but it was several minutes before she got herself under control. With a tearstained face, she looked up at him dolefully. "I thought once you turned middle-aged, you became too mature and wise to break down and cry like a lovesick adolescent."

Gary kissed her lightly on the forehead. "Cheer up. You've still got a few days left before you've got to turn wise and mature. If I were you, I'd make the most of it," he said with a grin.

"Have a few cries for me, too. I'm so middle-aged I've had to be on the wagon for years."

"I promise." She was true to her word. Reaching blindly for some more tissues, she started crying again.

Sam watched the young calf romp around the open pasture, stopping every now and then to graze on the fresh green grass. His mind drifted back a few months to that cold winter night in his barn when Joanna had watched him bring that calf into the world. He remembered the wide-eyed expression of awe on her face as she stood a little apart. . . .

Over the months she had stepped closer and closer to his world. If Gary Simms hadn't shown up two weeks ago, Joanna would be here beside him getting as big a thrill watching this calf as he was getting. Instead, she was sitting behind some desk in a little cubicle exuding confidence, delivering yet another winner of a campaign pitch. For the hundredth time he found himself wishing she had never gotten the impulsive romantic notion to come up to Brandon to test out new waters. Then he would never have known what he was missing. Now the knowing was driving him crazy. He was surprised none of his crew had mutinied yet; he surely was giving them enough reason. He was irritable and erratic, flying off the handle frequently. But his crew, and even Penelope, merely nodded their heads knowingly, their sympathetic smiles greeting his steely scowls. What did they know that he didn't?

He climbed onto the fence, a smile on his face as he spotted his daughter coming along down the road. She missed Joanna, too, almost as much as he did. It was the topic of conversation each night at the dinner table. *Have you heard anything from Jo? Why didn't she call? Why don't we call her?*

So many questions. So few answers. He tried to explain to his daughter that Joanna needed time without undue influence to sort things out.

What things? That was always the next question. Sam usually shrugged as answer to that one and then tried to move the conversation away from the subject of Jo.

He wanted nothing more than to say that she was coming back soon. In his heart that was exactly what he wanted to believe, but he couldn't make promises. He'd hoped she would call, his pride blocking his own desire to lift up that receiver, dial her New York number, and hear her voice. The truth was he was afraid he'd hear a tone of regret in her voice, mingled with an excitement and enthusiasm she wouldn't be able to hide.

"Hi, Sam."

"How was school today?"

"Okay. Heard from Jo?"

On Thursday morning, when Joanna woke up, for a moment she thought she was back in Brandon. At first she couldn't figure out why, and

167

then her radio alarm clock again blasted with the sound of birds. "Okay, sleepyheads. The birds have found their way to the city at last. Spring is here, folks. So rise and shine on this glorious, sunny Thursday and remember, Friday afternoon is just around the corner."

Joanna groaned, plunking the pillow over her head. Last night's prebirthday celebration with a few friends had given her the first morning hangover she'd had in almost a year. When she finally managed to crawl out of bed and make her way to the bathroom, she stared in her mirror and groaned again, this time with more heart.

After rubbing her bleary eyes, she looked at herself once more and decided that her thirtieth birthday had arrived with a depressing thud. *I've got office pallor, bloodshot eyes, worry lines creeping in at the corners of my eyes. I must be home,* she thought with finality.

Reaching the office, Joanna immediately noticed a new air around the place. She had a pretty good idea why.

She stopped in at Gary's office. Giving him a suspicious glance, she said, "I suppose it's not going to do any good if I tell you I don't want a surprise birthday party today."

"Is today your birthday? Hey, that's great, Jo. Happy birthday. Gee, I wish I'd known. Oh, yeah, you did mention something to me the other day. You can tell where my head is at."

"Gary."

He walked over to her and planted a kiss on her cheek.

"No point in begging, I guess." She sighed.

Gary grinned. "Come on, Jo. There's cause for celebration."

"Not the way I feel today," she grumbled. "If this is what it's like to enter my thirties, give me twenty-nine again any day."

"Honey, your birthday is just the icing on this celebration."

"Play that one again."

"Oops. I'm not supposed to play it even once."

"You mean the D and D account. It's no secret, Gary. Tom Bailey told me yesterday afternoon that he got the verbal okay. If that's the other reason for the celebration, then you get to share the table of honor with me. You did a terrific job, Gary. Did I tell you that already?"

"Every day for the past three weeks, Jo. And every day I followed it with 'You bring out the best in me.' It happens to be the truth, so I don't mind repeating it constantly."

"Well, we've almost got this one wrapped up. Another week or so, and my part will be finished. A little over schedule, but not too bad for someone who was out of practice."

"That's like saying Jim Rice gets out of practice between baseball seasons. You were just giving that brilliant mind of yours a needed respite before the next attack."

"Gary, I've got to admit the best part of being

back here is the daily boost you give my floundering ego."

"What happens to that ego next week?"

"That is the sixty-four-thousand-dollar question. How about giving me the answer as a birthday present?"

"That just might be arranged." He couldn't keep a wait-and-see smile from breaking out on his face.

"There's a mysterious look in those smiling eyes of yours, Mr. Simms. Something tells me more is brewing than you're letting on."

"Are you going to stand around my office all morning, lady? Last I heard, your birthday has not been designated a national holiday."

Joanna surveyed Gary for another few seconds as he pretended avid interest in a pink telephone message slip. Then she turned on her heels, knowing he was not going to give up any secrets.

At three o'clock the mystery began to unravel. When Joanna walked back into her office after a wild-goose chase to track down one of her misplaced storyboards, she was greeted by a round of cheers and quite a few hands extending champagne-filled plastic glasses in her direction. Corny as it felt to cry, especially knowing the "surprise" was coming, she shed a few tears anyway, smiling and reddening all at the same time.

"Thanks, folks. It's nice to turn thirty among friends . . . if you have to turn thirty." She laughed.

Gary was the one delegated to present her with the birthday gift from everyone there. For a moment, as Joanna stared at the large, beautifully wrapped box, she thought about the night Sam had brought her that beautiful dress. . . . She opened the box, blinking away an errant tear. Inside was a lovely handwoven shawl in shades of lilac, cream, and pale blue. She lifted it out, and in a gesture of gaiety that belied the wave of depression hitting her, she flung the shawl around her shoulders.

Doug Johnson, the more silent of the two partners in the firm, gave Joanna a warm handshake. Seven months ago he had been the one to warn her she might not have a job to come back to if she acted on what he viewed as a totally crazy scheme.

Now that she had secured the D & D account, he was more than willing to let bygones be bygones.

A couple of minutes later Joanna learned he was willing to do more than that. As he cleared his throat, she caught the glance of a beaming Gary Simms.

"Jo," Doug Johnson said in his auspicious speech-giving voice, "we at Bailey and Johnson do not believe in mere congratulations for jobs well done . . . as you already know, in view of your rise in this company."

Tom Bailey came over and put his arm around her. "Let's not beat around the bush, Doug," he said, drawing a bulky envelope out of his inside jacket pocket. "Not only is this a party to celebrate your birthday, Jo, but in this envelope you will find a more tangible expression of our gratitude for a job well done."

Joanna took the envelope. It was far too thick to contain nothing but a bonus check. She opened it a little warily. Last time she opened an official-looking envelope her whole life had turned topsy-turvy.

This time was no different. The check was there all right—a nice, fat bonus that would make her solvent again after seven months of watching her slender bank account grow steadily leaner. And the rest of the bulk concerned news that would turn her world upside down all over again.

CHAPTER TEN

The open envelope lay next to her phone on the small oak plant table in the studio apartment. Joanna stared at both each time she walked by. Twice now she had picked up the receiver, once going so far as to dial half the digits in Sam's phone number.

She munched on an apple, more to occupy herself than because she was hungry. The office staff had tried to ply her with champagne and the kinds of frozen hors d'oeuvres sold only in gourmet food stores. It all was very chic, but Joanna's stomach couldn't handle anything after she had opened the envelope from Tom Bailey.

She looked at the phone again now, going over a dozen speeches in her head. All of them sounded too pat or too disjointed. Her mind was swimming, and the apple was not helping the knot in her stomach. She set the fruit down and walked hesitantly over to the phone. They had to talk. Time was no longer an undefined quantity. A decision had to be made in a matter of three days. Joanna pushed aside pride, fear, and confusion.

The phone rang just as she reached out for the receiver again.

"Hello."

"Happy birthday, Jo."

"Sam!"

"For a minute there, dialing the phone, I was scared you might have forgotten my voice."

"You haven't done much to help me remember it," she reminded him.

"Yeah, I know. I decided to trade in my steel rod for a tree trunk with a little more give. Are you all right? You sound funny."

"I'm just swallowing a piece of apple."

"Oh." Sam paused. "How are things going?"

"Great."

"Jo . . . we don't seem to be doing much better on the phone today than we did three weeks ago."

"Oh, Sam," she whispered huskily into the phone.

"That's better." He laughed.

"No, it isn't. It's awful. I just don't know what to do. Every time I think I've got it all sorted out, somebody throws me a curve."

"Who threw the latest one?"

Joanna carried the phone over to the couch and sat down. "I was just offered a position as junior partner in the prestigious firm of Bailey and Johnson, Inc."

Sam inhaled slowly. "Quite a curve."

"Is that all you can say? Sam, there are no other junior partners at the agency. This is not just a token promotion for winning a new contract. The salary, the prestige, the power I would have—last year I would have been leaping into the air with joy."

"What are you doing now?"

"I'm lying on the couch, one hand pressed against my throbbing head, the other clutching my queasy stomach."

"Sounds as if you could use some good fresh mountain air," he said, trying for lightness.

"Look, Sam, I'm thirty years old today. I can't afford to waste time floundering around, trying to figure out what I want out of life. And I can't keep bouncing back and forth between two worlds. Despite what you might think, I don't love feeling like a volleyball. If I go back to Brandon, it has to be to stay. And if I remain here . . ."

"You know what I want. I love you, Jo."

He was the old Sam again: loving, gentle, sympathetic, his words caressing her in a warm embrace.

"Sam, I love you."

"Ayhup." He laughed softly.

"I love Penelope, too. I miss you both so much. I miss Calhoun. How is the old goat?"

"Come home and see for yourself."

"I thought you didn't want to pressure me."

"Can't help it. Calhoun keeps staring at me with such a forlorn expression every time I go over to check on him that I finally promised I'd do the best I could. Well, I've done it. Except to repeat once more . . . I love you, Joanna Winfield. My arms have been outstretched all this time, aching though they may be. So I decided the hell with pride and with walking around ranting and raving every day because you're gone. I don't want you to forget what's waiting for you . . . back home, Jo."

"Whichever way I turn, I feel I'm giving up something important to me, Sam."

"Life isn't simple. You should have learned that fast enough when you set out on your quest to find the simple life. There are always hidden problems, catastrophes, sacrifices. Jo, everyone, including me, wants it all. There's nothing wrong in that. It forces us to keep plugging, but the chances of really getting it all—well, that's another story. So you find yourself having to weigh your choices: the advantages, the disadvantages; the things you need badly, those you can manage without. I wish there were an easy answer, but in real life the answers are tough to come by."

"I'll have to come up with one by Monday, tough or not. Bailey is ready to call the sign painter first thing Monday morning to put my name up on the door to my plush new office."

"Well, I guess we'll both know by Monday whether I should buy you a new pair of work shoes."

"And the chickens. Don't forget the chickens," she whispered, her voice muffled.

"Jo. Jo, are you crying?"

"Chickens seem to make me teary lately. If you saw me now, Sam, I doubt you'd see a potential chicken farmer sitting here in her Ralph

176

Lauren business suit, pearl necklace and matching earrings."

"Didn't you once tell me about your uncle the chicken farmer?"

Tom Bailey was pulling out all the stops. When Joanna arrived in her office Friday morning, she found a sample book of carpet swatches, a half dozen brochures for top-of-the-line office furniture, and a memo from the man himself about an exciting new plum for her to start nibbling on—the Gardner fast food chain account.

Stretched across the surface of her desk were all the accoutrements of success. And she deserved this, she admitted to herself. The office on the top floor, the gold lettering on her door, the best accounts, the money—she had earned them all. Now was the time to turn in her chips and accept the prize.

"Good morning, Jo. Or do I have to start showing more respect now?" Gary quipped, popping his head inside her office.

"You knew about all this yesterday morning. You could have warned me."

"And spoiled that look on your face when you opened the envelope? Bailey told me only because your shift up means a promotion for me, too. Wipe that frown off your face. I step into this office whether you move up or out."

"Well, that's one less thing I'd have to feel guilty about." She sighed.

"I thought for sure yesterday you had made

your decision. It's a hell of a lot to turn down, Jo."

"No kidding." She lifted up a couple of furniture samples and tossed them over to Gary. "Take a look at what success will buy."

Gary bent down and retrieved the brochures from the floor. He flipped through them. "The light oak, definitely. You're not the mahogany type."

"You think I'm not a farmer type either, huh?"

Gary cocked his head and studied her thoughtfully. "Sure you are, Jo. You proved to me you can blend into Shangri-la as well as you fit in here, surrounded by mellow oak desks, plush carpeting, and a picture window overlooking the East River."

"Do you have to make this place sound so good?"

"You had a pretty terrific view out of your country cottage window, too, if I remember correctly."

"You remember correctly." She ran a finger over a carpet swatch. "I talked with Sam last night."

"Something tells me he wasn't ecstatic over your promotion."

"You have a nice touch for understatement, Gary. It was a toss-up for who sounded more miserable. But I think I won. Sam had philosophy on his side . . . probably picked it up from reading *The Farmer's Almanac.* Or else he's just less emotional."

"Or he may be counting on the fact that love is thicker than advertising," Gary told her.

"Don't let Bailey hear you say that," she said. "Anyway, I'm not so sure it's true. I've been in advertising a lot longer than I've been in love. Time has to have some bearing on all this, doesn't it? I'm used to this life, damn it. Even the work isn't that tough. Here I don't have to rise with the cracking of the dawn, chop wood till my arms ache, worry about rushing through my shower before the hot water runs out. I'm spoiled, Gary. That's the heart of it. And don't you think life's a picnic for a dairy farmer's wife. I'm not the kind of person to sit around darning socks. I'd want to be right at Sam's side, helping him. Next time a cow went into labor, I wouldn't be able to stand off, watching from across the barn. I'd have to pitch in. Why, what if Sam were off somewhere on business? I might even have to deliver a calf myself."

"All you'd have to give birth to here are some clever ideas," Gary pointed out.

"Exactly."

"Does this mean you've made up your mind?"

"Let's say I'm leaning heavily . . . but still weighing my choices."

"That's progress . . . I think."

When Gary left, Joanna walked over to her window and stared down at the midmorning traffic. No view of the East River here. Her eyes fell on an array of skyscrapers as she looked directly across the street. As she stood there, surveying her domain, it was hard to believe she

179

was the same woman who had scanned wondrous mountains less than a month ago. Sam's world seemed so far away now. This view was not nearly as gratifying, but it was familiar, easy to assimilate. Even its surprises didn't throw her.

Later that morning Tom Bailey's secretary called her. Tom wanted to show her the new office and discuss some plans with her.

Joanna stepped out of the elevator on the twenty-third floor. Not mountain air, but definitely rarefied. The top floor of the skyscraper exuded elegant grace. Soft pale gray carpeting, a deep, rich tone of charcoal on the walls, upholstered waiting-room furniture in tasteful gray-on-gray geometrics. Joanna, in her sophisticated black linen suit and pale gray silk shirt, blended right in as though the interior designer had included her costuming in the overall color scheme.

Tom gave her an admiring glance and then led her down the hall to an empty office.

"I thought you'd want to get a good look at it before you started picking out furniture. Of course, it will take some time to get everything you want, but I have the connections to put a rush on whatever you choose."

"Tom, I haven't even decided on taking the job yet."

"I've been in this business long enough to know when a deal is cinched, Jo."

"And I've been in the business long enough to

know that until you get a signature on the dotted line, don't go counting your chickens—"

What was the matter with her? Was she going to be haunted by chickens for the rest of her life?

"I'll give you my answer on Monday, as we agreed."

"Sure. Sure. Why don't you just take some time and look around? Come Monday, if I see your neat script on that dotted line, we've got a lot of work to do."

Tom Bailey left her in the empty office, shutting the door behind him. Joanna stood in the middle of the room, slowly turning a full revolution.

It was big all right. And the view of the East River was unobscured. She could even picture the mellow oak furniture, the soft leather couch, the large fern hanging beside the window, her jacket draped on the brass coatrack near the door. And she could see herself in her new swivel chair behind the executive-size desk.

As she opened the door to leave, Joanna saw that someone had scraped the old lettering off the glass panel. Everything was set for her to move in.

The rest of the day Joanna remained at her old desk, putting the finishing touches on the D&D ads. There was continual traffic in and out of her office all afternoon, people stopping by to congratulate her on her promotion. After pointing out to the first two or three of them that she hadn't decided whether or not she was taking the job, she found it easier simply to thank her well-wishers and leave it at that.

"Do you want some more roast beef, Jo?"

"No, thanks, Julie. It was great, but I'm stuffed." *At least she didn't serve chicken,* Joanna thought. She'd probably never be able to look another chicken breast in the eye without thinking about . . .

"You'll have to come see Jo's swank new office, hon. Tom Bailey's going all out."

"Hey, come on. My old office—which now becomes your royal domain—wasn't half-bad, Gary," Joanna said, getting up to help Julie clear the table.

"I've got some great ideas for Gary's new office," Julie piped in. "Only so far Gary hasn't agreed with a single one of them."

"I'm not into cerise, what can I tell you?" Gary shrugged good-naturedly.

"That's only the accent color. And it's really more plum than cerise."

"All this because she picked up two hundred yards of material that has . . . plum as the accent color."

"It would make great curtains. Your feelings won't be hurt, I hope," Julie said to Joanna, "but I always did think drapes would soften the windows in that office."

Joanna smiled. "When I first moved in, there were some hideous dark blue curtains. I got rid of them, then never got around to hanging up new ones. But you're right. Curtains would look nice in the office. Make it more homey."

As they settled down to coffee and homemade apple pie, Julie shot Gary a curious glance and then turned to Joanna.

"So what will you do with your . . . country place. Sell it?"

Gary frowned. Before Joanna had arrived for dinner, he'd told Julie not to bring up anything to do with Brandon. Joanna had called him Saturday afternoon to say she had decided to stay on at the agency. In a hesitant voice she told him it was a once-in-a-lifetime opportunity that she couldn't pass up. He thought of mentioning that marrying the man of her dreams could be viewed as the same once-in-a-lifetime opportunity, but he figured she was certainly bright enough to sort that one out for herself. She'd obviously decided advertising was thicker than love after all.

Julie ignored Gary's frown and continued. "It sounds like such a terrific spot. With your raise, you could probably swing it as a second home."

"I could, but I don't plan to. I'm going to sell it. Monday morning after I give Bailey the good news, I'm calling a realtor in Brandon and asking him to put it on the market."

"You don't sound too happy about it. That must have been a tough decision for you to make." Julie reached over and squeezed Joanna's shoulder.

"I still haven't gotten the courage to call Sam.

How do you tell the man you love that it just can't work out."

Gary looked up over his coffee cup. "The deal ain't sealed yet, kid. There's nothing to stop you from changing your mind."

"I'm scared. Maybe I'm a coward, but I'm opting for success. I spent seven months learning incredible things up in Brandon, Vermont, but I always had to stave off feeling inept and incompetent every step of the way. Add to that the fact that if I went back, I'd have to learn how to be a dairy farmer and a mother, not to mention having to cope with the true rigors of country life minus all my earlier romantic notions, and my nice, swank office on the twenty-third floor of a skyscraper sounds luxurious beyond belief. Sometime I'll tell you a few of my more catastrophic adventures . . . when the pain wears off a little."

Stepping out of her apartment building, Joanna almost decided to take the bus instead of cramming into the morning rush-hour subway. In her creamy beige dress and matching blazer, she stood little chance of arriving at work without any telltale signs of her trip. Then she remembered that a bus ride had started this whole dilemma in the first place. She walked the two blocks to the subway station.

The platform was so crowded that when the train pulled up and the doors opened, Joanna was propelled inside, her feet barely touching the ground in the process. She was one of the lucky ones to find a subway strap to cling to. She fell against the man beside her as the train lurched forward. Apologizing, she quickly looked away as the heavyset man grinned broadly, the message clear he wouldn't mind a second lurch.

Today was the big day. She still hadn't called Sam, but after she'd spoken with Bailey, casting her die, she'd have to face all the repercussions of her decision. She'd talked to herself all morning about the pros of staying. Everything sounded logical, reasonable, reassuring. She was convinced she was making the only realistic choice possible.

And then two things happened. First, trying to avoid eye contact with the insistent man beside her, she cast her eyes upward, pretending an interest in the poster ads along the walls of the subway car. There she spotted a picture of cows grazing in a pasture with the sign above them: "Milk is for you." All at once a fierce wave of utter homesickness swept over her. Here she was on her way to accept the position of junior partner in one of the top advertising agencies in the city, and she was staring at those cows as if they were the most wonderful things she'd ever seen.

Oh, my God, she whispered under her breath, a thread of perspiration beading her brow. Maybe there really was a fairy godmother looking out for her, guiding her in the right direction. "Milk is for you." She laughed, ignoring the surreptitious stares. Suddenly those words made everything crystal clear. All her nagging doubts, her fears, her equivocating thoughts vanished with some adman's clever message for selling the consumer another product.

The ad had certainly worked. Never had she craved milk more than at that moment. Milk from a dairy farm up in Vermont. In fact, the biggest, the best dairy farm in these parts. Ayhup. That was exactly what she wanted.

Then, as if she needed more incentive, the second deciding factor occurred: The man beside her reached across and pinched her bottom. Even though she glared at him with a cuttingly scornful look, in her heart this was the coup de grace of convincing arguments for getting off that train at the next stop and calling the Greyhound terminal to find out when the next bus left for Brandon.

Here she was again, acting on another crazy, impulsive decision. Only this time it felt completely right. She was going home. At the ripe old age of thirty Joanna had finally realized what truly mattered to her.

She'd left Bailey sputtering on the phone. He probably never would get over that call. She'd told him she was down at the Greyhound bus terminal, and she had made the decision to go with the chickens after all.

Gary, amazingly enough, wasn't really surprised by the news. In fact, he sounded relieved. When Joanna asked him why, he told her this was the first time in nearly four weeks that she sounded unequivocably happy. He also confided that Julie thought she was crazy to choose a view of the East River over Shangri-la.

The four-hour bus ride seemed interminable. She was filled with an excitement and anticipation not unlike that first trip up to Brandon. But this time she was not cushioned in false, romantic notions and fantasies of the simple life. The very fact that she had so much to learn, so much to discover made it all the better. She was finally giving herself the chance to accomplish goals that had real meaning and value for her. And while she was learning and growing, Sam would be beside her, telling her the difference between planes and rasps, teaching her how to birth a cow, showing her the beauties and wonders of nature.

When she stepped off the bus in town, Joanna was stunned by the number of people who came over and welcomed her back. Somehow her image as a stranger in a strange land had disappeared. She walked down the street, a new and wonderful feeling sweeping over her. She belonged here. The shops, the people, the old movie theater, Bob Webster's hardware store— they all were familiar, all part of her world. She wanted to run down the road, kissing everyone she passed.

And then she spotted her old beat-up red pickup truck parked a couple of doors down from the hardware store. Bob Webster tapped on his window to get her attention. He was jangling a set of keys in his hand.

"Sam left these with me," Bob said as Joanna walked into the shop. "He said to tell you he wasn't trying to spoil you by leaving your truck here for you to drive home, but he figured this way you could take the solar panels back with you. Give me a minute, and I'll load them on for you."

"Hold on, Bob. What panels? I didn't order any panels. We—we talked about them but I wasn't—" She started to say she wasn't even sure she was really coming back, much less ready to carry out the plans for her greenhouse.

"Sam called me first thing Saturday morning and told me to go ahead with the order, Jo. If you don't want the panels I'll—"

"No, I want them all right." The question was: How could Sam have been so sure she wanted them?

Bob loaded the panels into the bed of the pickup and Joanna slid into the worn front seat, which at that moment felt worlds better than the plush swivel chair Tom Bailey had insisted she try out last Friday. She gave the old truck a friendly pat. It purred like a newborn kitten for her as she turned the key in the ignition.

Sam's new truck was in her driveway, loaded with lumber. When Joanna opened her front door, she was met with a loud hammering sound. She stared in wide-eyed wonder at the gaping hole where the back wall of her house had once stood.

"Sam Chase, what the hell is going on here?" she screamed above the noise.

188

Sam, poised on a ladder, large wooden board in hand, turned his head around in her direction.

"Don't just stand there, Jo. Slip into your work shoes and give me a hand."

She walked closer, paying no attention to his orders. "What are you doing?"

He sighed, carefully easing the board back down to the floor. Then he turned on the ladder to face her fully.

"I'm giving you a start on that greenhouse."

Joanna smiled, her eyes filling with tears. "Oh, Sam, I'm such a dope."

"I'd never call you a dope, Jo. Although for a while there I have to admit you had me a bit worried. But I figured you'd come around, being the fast learner that you are. So I thought I'd get the cabin fixed up a little . . . actually I wasn't counting on your coming back without notice . . . I'd planned to have more done than this natural air conditioning. Until we get married, I thought you might like a few more creature comforts—as well as space. Go check out the bathroom."

Joanna eyed him curiously, then turned and walked into the bathroom.

"Wait a sec. This goes with the new addition." Sam handed her a small gift-wrapped package.

The new addition was a beautiful bathtub, installed right beside her shower. Inside the package was a large bottle of bath oils called Country Mist.

"But, Sam, I told you I was seriously thinking about taking that job. I told you—"

"I told you that I love you. And you told me you love me. You'd never said that before . . . in quite that way. I figured you'd come to your senses in time."

"I—I did. I—I do," she stammered, putting her arms around him.

"Sounds as if you've got your lines already memorized. Welcome home, Jo."

He held her so close she felt she was melting right into him. It was the best feeling she'd had since she boarded that Greyhound bus out of Brandon a few weeks ago.

"Oh, Sam, I am home. I really am."

"Of course you are." He grinned and planted a moist loving kiss on her lips. "After all, you can take the girl out of the country, but you can't take the country out of the girl."

"Ayhup," she said and kissed him back again. And then again, more deeply.

"What do you say we go back to the farm and tell Penelope you're here to stay?"

"I thought she was officially changing her name to Jane when she turned sixteen. I sent her a birthday card last week addressed to Jane Chase."

"Seems my daughter has come to some decisions these past few weeks, too. When she turned sweet sixteen, she decided after all that Penelope was the name that fitted her best."

Joanna laughed as Sam put his arm around her.